M. M. Misevicius, is an artist and a dreamer. He is a general contractor by day and a writer by night.

This is the first of several books the author has written, including *Among Lions*, a riveting prequel that intricately explores the fascinating origins of *Hearts of Men*.

For my mother, the best writer in the family and my inspiration.

# M. M. Misevicius

# HEARTS OF MEN

AUSTIN MACAULEY PUBLISHERS™
LONDON • CAMBRIDGE • NEW YORK • SHARJAH

**Copyright © M. M. Misevicius (2019)**

All rights reserved. No part of this publication may be reproduced, distributed, or transmitted in any form or by any means, including photocopying, recording, or other electronic or mechanical methods, without the prior written permission of the publisher, except in the case of brief quotations embodied in critical reviews and certain other non-commercial uses permitted by copyright law. For permission requests, write to the publisher.

Any person who commits any unauthorized act in relation to this publication may be liable to criminal prosecution and civil claims for damages.

This is a work of fiction. Names, characters, businesses, places, events, locales, and incidents are either the products of the author's imagination or used in a fictitious manner. Any resemblance to actual persons, living or dead, or actual events is purely coincidental.

**Ordering Information:**
Quantity sales: special discounts are available on quantity purchases by corporations, associations, and others. For details, contact the publisher at the address below.

**Publisher's Cataloging-in-Publication data**
Misevicius, M. M.
Hearts of Men

ISBN 9781947353312 (Paperback)
ISBN 9781947353305 (Hardback)
ISBN 9781645364078 (ePub e-book)

Library of Congress Control Number: 2019935781

www.austinmacauley.com/us

First Published (2019)
Austin Macauley Publishers LLC
40 Wall Street, 28th Floor
New York, NY 10005
USA

mail-usa@austinmacauley.com
+1 (646) 5125767


20200923

# Table of Contents

| | |
|---|---:|
| 1 Charlie | 3 |
| 2 Joe | 7 |
| 3 Simon | 12 |
| 4 Clive | 17 |
| 5 Neil | 22 |
| 6 Roebuck | 27 |
| 7 Willy | 31 |
| 8 Into the Wilderness | 40 |
| 9 Not Alone | 48 |
| 10 Insight | 56 |
| 11 Recourse | 63 |
| 12 In the Mist | 72 |
| 13 Seeking Allies | 79 |
| 14 Back South | 86 |
| 15 Unification | 93 |
| 16 J. Oskar Emmlington | 102 |
| 17 Know Your Enemy | 109 |
| 18 A Tiny Light Amidst Infinite Dark | 119 |
| 19 Above the Hollow | 128 |
| 20 The Storm | 136 |
| 21 What If? | 147 |
| 22 A Long Time | 154 |
| 23 Hope | 162 |
| 24 Death from Above | 167 |
| 25 Alone | 172 |
| 26 Methods of Mayhem | 178 |
| 27 Liberation | 186 |

In every walk with nature
one receives far more than he seeks.

~ John Muir

"Tell the gentlemen with the organization that payment shall be prompt upon reception of the packages and not to bother me with details of the procedure."

**Several months later...**

# 1
# Charlie

Sunlight pours through the windowpane of Charlie's breakfast nook. It saturates a thick stack of plain white paper, leaving it luminescent within its bright haze there atop the table. The place meant for having the first-and-most-important meal of the day is, in fact, rarely used for this purpose. But instead for housing laptops, printers, ink-cartridges, notebooks, manila envelopes, and just about anything else one would use to methodically put one's imagination to glorious use; for partaking in the unforgiving pursuit of vindication. Charlie even has a small pile of publishing self-help books to aid in his tireless efforts. The space is utilized to bring some of Charlie's fantasies to life. Where he can obsessively unpack just a fraction of the imprisoned scenarios that whirl around up in his over-active, complex mind and attach them together into stories.

Outside his cluttered little home, it is a gorgeous Tampa morning. Various birds fly up and down, chasing and swooping as they play. Charlie stands, arms crossed, with a cup of steaming coffee in his left hand. The young man is of average height and weight with mid-length black hair, arranged in a side-parted haircut and his eyes are dark, not only their particular shade of brown, but the accompanying bags underneath. He wears beige khakis and a white, long-sleeved undershirt. He squints as he looks through the bright, uncovered window of the nook. He winces through the sunshine, watching the swallows fly sporadically from the blue sky above and into the green shelter of a nearby red cedar tree.

He ponders his main character's destiny and how he will align with it.

Charlie has been working for quite some time on what to write and what not to write. In fact, he has been pondering all spring. Stockpiling ideas and angles. He's written seven books of fiction, four full-length novels, one novella, and two novelettes. He doesn't count his short stories within his total sum, but he should.

Now, he's gone back to his first story... His very first. It consists of fifty-thousand words, *roughly*, and after being read by trusted friends and knocked around the publishing industry—where it has been pushed into the slush-pile, lost, dropped, kicked, stepped on, picked up, wiped off, flipped through, read, and returned—for four years, he has finally revisited it. No matter how long he watches the birds or fills his cup or even how many times light shines through his window, Charlie is perplexed. Is it the wrong timing? Bad luck? It had been a few years since he had read through it. Perhaps his growth as a writer should be applied. He isn't certain, but he questions himself about the only issue there could possibly be. Can his story *really* be *that* flawed structurally? He can think of no other reason why it is overlooked time and again and intends to fix it.

In the years that followed his first piece, he noticed something, something significant, when he wrote. He couldn't see it in the first book...somewhere within his second one...the structure began to build itself...naturally. The proper grammar simply came. Run-on sentences dispelled and so did his overly descriptive style, without sacrificing depth. Charlie was growing all the time, and he knew it.

In his backyard, he notices a red piece of material or…*something*. It's about twenty-five yards away, in front of a row of well-manicured bushes. The ones at the back of his lot, below a line of trees.

He sits down, picks up a pencil, and stares at a blank page in front of him. He stares for one minute, then two. His eyes seem to burn. He writes, 'FUCK!' Charlie rises abruptly from the table, cheeks filled to capacity with oxygen, and exhales steadily and methodically. "Fuuuuuckkk," he whispers, as he lets the air out. "What is that?" One of the many troubles of being over-analytical is that you can't allow a piece of foreign, red material to just lie there in your otherwise perfect little backyard uninspected, before discarding it in its allocated recycling bin.

If it were last autumn, the 'red menace' in his yard wouldn't have bothered him. He'd had enough to keep him busy, but that was before the 'breakup.' He had *her* to occupy him and wouldn't have noticed a red *thing* on his lawn, let alone cared.

Charlie has re-written about ninety percent of a beautiful book about a group of brothers thrown into conflict with unrelenting evil. He'd thought of this story years ago; writing it in his head over and over and researching until finally putting his story to hard copy and now he's back to it and almost finished, he tries in vain to resist distraction, but looks at a picture set on his table. A child, himself at seven years old, if that. He then looks to a couple of piles of influential books. On top of the nearest pile, lies '*The Shack*' by W.M. Paul Young, then there is 'Life of Pi' by Yann Martel and '*The Road*' by Cormac McCarthy is underneath that. He looks outside again to the red fleck and then over to another pile and to a trio of old beloved classics. One is much thinner than the other. He glances at 'The Legend of Sleepy Hollow' by Washington Irving and then the epic 'Alice's Adventures in Wonderland' by Lewis Carroll, followed by the short story 'Dracula's Guest' by Bram Stoker.

"Alright, what is it?" says Charlie. He crosses the kitchen to the side deck, where he jogs down the steps and around to his backyard.

Charlie is young and fit. He looks more at home outdoors, walking amongst natural, green surroundings than sitting at a jumbled, make-shift desk indoors.

He thinks about his nearly completed re-write as he goes. His mind is aggravated as the distance between he and his work station widens and is less interested in the red thing outside now that he is on his way to it and not inside where he longs to be. He approaches the mystery. As Charlie picks it up, he realizes that it's a small Nazi German flag.

"What the hell are you doing here?" he asks the flag. He examines its pitch-black lines, bright white circle, and blood-red backdrop.

Before turning to head back inside flag in hand, he scans the endless green landscapes beyond his backyard. Nothing but old wooden, split rail fencing separating vast, open fields. Suddenly, he hears a series of snaps from the large bushes behind him.

Before he can spin around to uncover the source of the disturbance, he feels a blunt, heavy impact on the top of his head. He falls to the ground. A sharp pain travels through his body. Charlie has entered dreamland.

# 2
# Joe

A mound of sawdust lay underneath a workbench. A pile much larger than what he would usually allow. Especially for someone who keeps such an organized workshop. The walls of the shed are lined with shelves, on which are plenty of tools and bits of hardware. Above most of them are labels with names and dimensions. In the back corner there are two brand-new, well-detailed doghouses. They are positioned side-by-side, complete with windows and even doors that can move in and out by spring-activated hinges. Both have cream-colored vinyl sidings with dark-brown asphalt shingles. The one on the left has red shutters while the one on the right has blue.

In the adjacent corner, atop a rugged plywood counter, sits a radio with a bent-wire hanger, drawing in fractured radio waves. Narrow rays of light pierce through scattered nail holes and the only window the structure has. Within the light dance countless tiny particles of dust.

They swish and swirl slowly as they descend to the coarse concrete floor. A man's voice from the radio abruptly belts through the mild drone of crackling static:

"It's not that I don't believe in the existence of aliens altogether! It's just that *I've* never seen one… You're listening to Pat Crystal…CJLP 98.9 FM… Up next, a man named Tim Adams, from just around the way, who claims he's been to hell and back again… A story of righteous perseverance against wicked forces of the highest power… Stay tuned."

Just then, an old white pick-up truck pulls down the short dirt driveway.

It's a beautiful summer day. Not a cloud in the sky as birds chirp from every angle.

Further down the driveway, to the truck's far left, is the shed. It's long been used as a modest workshop.

It is small in size, about six-hundred feet squared, at best and is very old, as evidenced by a maple tree growing almost from right underneath its foundation, along its side and up high, several feet above. The exterior is all together shoddy. It's a sheen-less shade of brown with a tarnished, galvanized steel roof. On the right side, opposite the out-building and across the driveway, is a quaint bungalow that certainly shows *its* years too. Nearly as many as those of the shed. The house is mediocre, plain, and ordinary. There are no neighboring houses in any direction, as far as the eye can see. Only open fields. But a few tall trees tower here and there. They are accompanied by low numbers of bushes and the scarce ruins of old log fences scantily divide the fields, this truly is 'God's country,' the townspeople would say.

The truck stops just past a mailbox fashioned to look like a birdhouse. Out hops a young man with a medium build. He is about five-feet ten or so and has a slightly dark complexion, dark hair, brown eyes, and a five o'clock shadow, though it's still only morning, upon a close look, dew covers with its coat of shiny beads, the mailbox and just about everything else.

The man is dressed in work clothes: dark overalls, a black baseball cap, and a red-and-white plaid shirt with the sleeves rolled all the way up to his biceps.

There is a worn-out chrome-cased measuring tape hooked to the left-side pocket of his overalls, and he wears beat-up, tan colored steel-toed boots. He opens the mailbox, but there is nothing out of the ordinary. Typical junk mail, flyers, and what not. He disregards all of it except the last envelope, which says:

Joe A. Smith
#9 Whippoorwill Lane
Greenborough N.Y.

He opens it and unfurls the piece of paper inside. It's another flyer. This one, though, appears handmade and photocopied. It reads:

**"As Springtime has come to its end to bring about a new summer, we are respectively sending out this little notice to our loyal customers as a reminder, to spay and/or neuter their furry little friends… and the big ones too! Also, we are holding a pet-food super-sale from now all the way to July 4$^{th}$.**
**Sincerely,**
**Peggy Bloom and your friends at the old 'Border town Pet Market'."**

As Joe reads the letter, he can't help but smile and revel at just how much he loves living right there in his small town in upstate New York. 'Way upstate,' as some of the locals would say. He thinks about how simple and pleasant life truly is for him and everyone there… For people like Peggy Bloom.

Joe climbs into his truck, pulls it over down by the workshop, and goes inside. He works away as the weatherman on the radio explains the day, "On this lovely morning, expect no change… Clear skies and warm breezes."

He looks up to an intricately crafted sign that hangs above the radio and on the wall:

Smith's Carpentry
Quality Craftsmanship at Realistic Prices
315-KL5-2046

With the slightest smile and a glint in his eye, Joe averts his eyes back down and continues creating his newest birdhouse.

That night, after doing the dishes from his dinner of one, Joe sits on his living room couch with a beer. Work clothes exchanged for more casual wear. Jeans and a white t-shirt with an, unbuttoned, flannel blue-and-green plaid shirt. He flips around the television channels between a couple of baseball games, the Discovery channel, and National Geographic while playing with his pet dog Kalyden, a full-grown yellow Labrador with a blue collar.

"You're into baseball, aren't ya?" asks Joe. The excited dog rolls on the couch beside him as if to say, 'Yes, definitely, whatever *you* like, I *love*.'

"I'll tell you what," says Joe, "I'll go get a second coat of varnish on my little canary condo and you can come with me." The rambunctious animal barks, and with that, they head out toward the workshop.

Outside, the dog runs on ahead of his owner and past the shed. "No hunting!" calls Joe.

"The last time you brought me that poor little bluebird, I didn't appreciate it at all. There's got to be other things to do out here for fun, right?"

The distracted dog doesn't acknowledge a word and continues on his path to God-knows-where.

He will often bolt to the fields once outside, and that's just fine with his best friend. He is a relatively good companion and always comes back before too long.

Joe opens the door to his shop and flicks on the lights. To his dismay, his latest project is toppled over on its side. As well some tools look out of place. *Something isn't right*, he thinks. Instantaneously, he is struck on his head by a hard, merciless blow.

Before he can figure out by what or who, he hits the concrete floor with a crash. A pipe wrench does the same. Joe is unconscious and the lights of the workshop immediately turn off. A moment later, his dog comes running over through the black of night. There is a muffled yip, and all is silent.

# 3

# Simon

With rain falling steadily upon most of the city of Seattle, countless workaday citizens hustle and bustle on the streets, in and out of cars and buildings. The odd person carries an umbrella. Most of them do not. The weather won't stop anyone. Too busy. Especially in this day and age. The sidewalks seem even busier than usual. It is lunch-hour. *12 o'clock sharp on another lovely day*, thinks Simon to himself as he exits the rather lucrative computer software company in which he works. Well, lucrative for C.E.O.s, executives and bosses... Not for Simon. He is just a tech support agent.

*Where to have lunch?* He wonders as he looks down the block and then upward. The need for an umbrella doesn't even cross his mind as he squints to see beyond the skyscrapers and into the gray sky. He starts on his route looking for a restaurant he has never tried. *Somewhere different today*, for a change, he affirms. Finally, he spots the spot, and quite literally too. It's a small spot between a bakery shop and a bookstore and is actually called '*The Spot.*' *Must be new*, he ponders.

Simon arrives at the corner of the street nearly diagonal to his freshly discovered destination, where he is bumped accidentally from behind by an old woman in an outfit that could only be described as outdated, unless it were 1955. But she is elderly, so her style of dress looks endearing and rather charming even if it *is* 2012. The woman, without skipping a beat, blurts out a small laugh.

"Oh dear, I'm sorry young man," she says.

"No, no, *my* apologies miss. Fine day, isn't it?" asks Simon, as he spins around. He even tips an imaginary hat, winks his right eye and smiles, revealing his perfect teeth.

Strongly believing a person should dress for the job they want, Simon is wearing a sharp navy-blue, three-piece suit and shiny dress shoes. He rubs the excess water from his very short blond hair and futilely wipes his glasses on his sleeve. He stands quite tall beside the woman of nearly average height.

"Ohhh, it's a daisy, just delightful!" she replies.

The crosswalk light changes from the orange hand to the white stickman.

Simon puts out his arm.

"May I?" he asks.

"Certainly," answers the woman.

They cross the street.

"Well, I'm headed right, and you?" asks Simon.

"Straight ahead. I am to visit my granddaughter at a place for tea, just down that way."

And with that, he strikes a bow, bringing his thoughtful assistance to a grand close.

"Have a fine day my lady!"

The woman chuckles.

"You as well my dear, and a fine day to you too!"

They exchange smiles and set out on their separate ways.

The Spot is four units down the block. Just as Simon passes the bakery, the door swings open. A man holding a confection box walks out aggressively, slamming right into Simon.

"Hey, fuck you buddy!" exclaims the stranger, very loudly and with great hostility.

The stranger hustles by, quite frustrated.

"Yes, not a problem," says Simon as he picks up his glasses from the drenched sidewalk. "Very nice... Yeah, courteous," he mumbles as he wipes off the lenses.

Shaking his head, he enters the restaurant.

'*Please Seat Yourself,*' reads the sign inside, so he does. The place is reasonably clean. The walls are heavily decorated with posters and framed pictures. There is typical retro Coca-Cola signage and old Campbell's Soup advertisements.

It is the kind of joint that has a black and white John. F. Kennedy portrait right beside a colorful cartoon drawing of a coffee bean wearing a cowboy hat and riding a mechanical bull. Obscure arrangements of pictures cover almost every square inch of vintage floral wallpaper, in no specific order and of no particular theme.

Simon looks at a poster of a kitten desperately clinging onto a clothesline, the caption reads: 'Hang in there.' The framed one beside it is a picture of Princess Diana and Nancy Reagan at an upscale social gala. Whomever designed the inside of the restaurant appears to have been well aware of their mission to plant the diminishing by-gone era of homey middle America right there in the heart of the booming tech industry of the pacific northwest.

The waitress arrives, taking her newest patron a bit off-guard.

"Hello sunshine! What can me getcha?" asks the woman in her late forties. She's ready to write on the pad of paper held out in front of her apron.

"Hello, umm... what's good?" asks Simon, perking up in his chair.

"Well, lotsa specials darlin', and it's *all* good," claims the server.

"Alright... Well... I'm easy...surprise me," says Simon.

"Okay hun, you sure you trust me to pick your lunch?"

"Sure do... There's lots of specials, and it's all good, right? And I'll start with a coffee please."

The server laughs.

"It is! Alright... A coffee, comin' right up," she says with a smile.

Simon carefully cleans the lenses of his glasses with a napkin and continues looking at all the interesting pictures and newspaper clippings hung about The Spot. The place certainly doesn't fit with most other downtown Seattle diners, but it's growing on Simon already.

The server arrives in good haste with a 'real' crabmeat sandwich, a house salad with raspberry vinaigrette dressing, his aforementioned coffee, and a glass of water

"Now, how's *this* for a surprise?" she asks.

Simon's gazing at a cartoon drawing of a fried egg stepping onto the moon from a space shuttle. The caption above the caricature reads: "Now this is what *I* call sunny-side up!" he turns to his lunch with a smile.

"Perfect," he answers. "I wouldn't have it any other way."

"On a day like this, I just hope the water isn't offensive." He looks his damp clothes over briefly and laughs. "Enjoy," says the server cheerfully.

Simon does and tips her generously afterward.

He arrives back at his cubicle shortly before 1 o'clock and works at his computer for about three hours. Stopping only to call his sister to ask how she's feeling and tell her he loves her and will see her soon, but to his disappointment, she didn't answer. At 4 o'clock, with a stretch and a yawn, he shuts his system down and grabs his jacket.

A short time later, he is walking through the dank, ever-darkening maze that is one of the building's many parking lots. He stops briefly to say hi and donate a couple of dollars to a homeless man lying by a stairwell. Feeling bittersweet about the transaction, he walks for a while amidst the dark of the gray cemented underground, the lighting is terrible, and the rainy overcast only worsens it. Finally, he arrives at his vehicle, but as he puts his key into the car door lock, there is a sudden commotion behind him. It is the sound of a revving engine and screeching tires, followed by rushing feet. Before he can turn around for a look, he feels an acute pain in his head and then his body. In no time, for Simon, the parking lot turns completely black.

# 4
# Clive

The steel rafters there were heavily coated with dust and cobwebs. Just below them hung a large scoreboard that flickered '2–1' with an effort best described as lackluster.

"Off the glass and out!" Clive yelled as the clock quickly wound down to thirteen seconds remaining. He stood behind the hockey players' bench filled with juveniles. They appeared even sadder than the scoreboard chugging along above center ice. Clive, in a pair of faded blue jeans and an un-buttoned beige corduroy blazer with elbow patches, looked very much to fit the part of a coach with his hands on his hips and dark hair combed just so. A bit young for such a responsibility, but not too young.

The seconds continue to tick down and so does Clive's tenure as head coach of the Jr. 'A' Red Ridge Riders. He looked on as his team failed to capture the pivotal two points that would have propelled them to their first play-off appearance in eleven years.

Once the arena was just about empty, Clive rounded the corner to the back entrance, where he was greeted rather solemnly by the Riders' general manager.

"Tough loss," said the G.M.

"I heard that," replied Clive sheepishly.

"Look Clive... You're what? Twenty-nine, thirty? There'll be more opportunities... Don't give up, you'll go places!"

"Thanks, Rodg."

"It's not your fault. You gave us a good three years, but we have got to shake it up. Our club needs changes in a lot of areas!"

"That's okay, I understand," said Clive.

That hurt, but he had always been a winner, never a poor sport. The young man had always bounced back. He was top of his class and an adept athlete. Clive had great potential, but in such a small town, there were not always enough open doors. Clive's plans were to continue with his determination intact, something would come up.

Two years rolled by, and Clive kept himself financially sound by working at a used sports equipment store in Portland. All the while keeping contact with local statewide sports teams: hockey, football, baseball... whichever. Whenever a team needed a coach or an assistant coach, Clive would apply.

His determination remained mostly in check, but he felt that maybe he was wasting his time, maybe there weren't enough teams within Oregon, or maybe he just wasn't qualified anymore.

Clive stands behind the counter of the sports store steadily drawing doodles: a transparent cube, a happy face, an eye, figure eights, scribbles and so on.

Stewart, Clive's co-worker, jogs up from the baseball equipment aisle and joins him behind the counter.

"Hey, man," says the young black man in disbelief. "You believe that guy?"

"What guy?" asks Clive.

"That guy!" replies Stewart, pointing him out with a smirk. "The kid thinks that baseball isn't a *real* sport, and he is *in* the baseball equipment section! I mean... I don't know!"

"Hmmm," ponders Clive.

"Yeah man, he said *baseball* is the only sport where doing a good job thirty percent of the time is considered playing well."

"Interesting point Stu."

"Man, WHAT?"

"I love baseball, but that's kind of an interesting point of view, that's all I'm sayin'."

"Man, shut up!" exclaims Stewart, playfully.

Just then, a little boy, no more than nine or so, runs up to the counter.

"Excuse me, sir? I can't find any left-handed junior-sized hockey sticks," says the boy.

"Follow me," orders Clive. He directs the boy to the hockey sticks.

"Ya know what? You're in luck!" he says as he hands the little boy the last left-handed junior.

"Wow! It's perfect. How much?" asks the boy while looking it over. Clive points to the price displayed on the rack.

"Um, thirty-nine dollars, plus tax."

"Oh, uhh... Okay," replies the boy as he looks to his toes.

"What's wrong?" asks Clive.

"Well, my mom," says the boy as he points out of the store to a bench in the center of the mall to a woman looking less than presentable. "My mom said that all she can afford to pay is twenty dollars, and from my piggy bank I only have eleven dollars and sixty-two cents, and that only makes," the boy pauses. "Thirty-one dollars and sixty-two cents all together."

He tells Clive, as if he wouldn't have known the math on his own.

"Ohhh, boy," says Clive. "How long have you been saving for?"

"Since Christmas."

"It's just turned summer."

"I know," says the boy, "but my dad comes over sometimes and says he really, really needs money."

"Ah, I see. Alright, tell you what kiddo, when you leave here, I want you to put that money in your pocket and don't tell anyone that you have it. Okay?"

"Oh, okay." The boy turns around and heads toward the exit.

"Hey!" calls Clive. "You're gonna forget your new stick!"

"What?" asks the boy.

"Your new stick," repeats Clive.

"YOU'RE KIDDING!" he shouts, now beaming ear to ear.

"I would never kid," Clive hands the little boy his new hockey stick.

"Thank you mister, thank you! Thank you!"

"My pleasure. Hey, what color of tape do you need? You can't use a stick without tape."

The boy looks at Clive as if he'd officially lost his mind.

"Uh. Blue, to match the lettering," quickly exclaims the boy.

"Good choice," agrees Clive, "here you go," he grabs a roll of blue tape from a nearby shelf and tosses it to the boy, who catches it nervously with stick in hand, as if both items are made of rare, precious materials *so* delicate, they would shatter should they fall to the floor. With an enormous smile, the boy runs off. Clive returns to the counter and the phone rings immediately.

"Super Star Sports," he answers upon picking it up.

He glances over to Stewart, who had just wrapped up a passionate debate with the aforementioned teenager in the baseball aisle and is heading in his direction.

"What? No, well...yes! Yes, I guess I have dropped off about three or four, yeah! Yep...okay, tomorrow at 12:45... For an interview. I'll be there with bells on! Thank *you* sir, thank you. B'bye," Clive hangs up the phone and notices Stewart staring closely at him.

"A coaching job?"

"You betcha, Stu!" Stewart continues to stare. "What?" says Clive with put-on disdain.

*"He's got an interesting point,"* says Stewart sarcastically.

The Trail blazer basketball clock on the wall above the side door that leads directly outside reads 10:15 p.m. Clive finishes the inventory alone and pays the balance of his donated hockey stick and roll of tape. He proceeds to shut down the store, and shortly after, all is set. He turns off the lights, locks the door behind him, double checks it, and steps outside onto the dimly lit sidewalk of the mall's back parking lot. As soon as he steps off the curb and onto the road, a black Mercedes Benz cargo van with no windows pulls up fast behind him from the shadows and, in an instant, the side door of the Metris slides open. Two sets of arms reach out from inside and grab Clive, A black bag is thrown over his head, and they quickly pull him in.

Within the darkness and on his back, an immense pain enters Clive's body and just like that, he and the van are gone.

# 5

# Neil

It had been three days since the last time Neil worked at the call center. He has been getting over a cold recently and is not enthusiastic about ever returning at all.

"It can't be that bad, can it?" asks his pal Tom. Neil stares at the beer in front of him. The two had had a barbeque on Neil's back deck and been there almost all afternoon enjoying the summer sunshine.

"It's demoralizing" replies Neil. "It takes a toll on a person emotionally. For the longest time, I loved it. I mean, I really did love it. But the more you listen, the more you hear, it starts to leave you so…empty."

"Yeah, but you're, y'know…helping people," says Tom.

"I know, I know. It's just, it never ends. There're so many hurt people, the sadness can just envelope you. Sorta like it's contagious, the sadness, I mean. You can only hear so many awful stories before it seems hopeless. And it's so simple. It's always someone being cold and abusive to someone else."

"Move over world peace, as the apocalypse sets in. You goin' back soon?" asks Tom with a laugh.

"Yeah, The Crisis Centre and I, well, I guess I'm in it to win it… I'll do what I've always done… put on a happy face and rise to the call," says Neil. He grins a bit at his cheap, but well-placed pun.

"Nice, well I know what'll cheer ya up!"

"Oh, yeah. What's that?" asks Neil, more making a statement than actually asking a question.

"One word: Sara!"

Neil smirks.

"Geez Tommy, y'know I haven't been on a date since... I can't remember, and now you get me roped into this one? And a blind date at that!"

"Will you listen to yourself? It's for your own good. Louise said she's a great girl, and pretty too!"

"Well, I appreciate it Tommy, I do. The whole thing just makes me nervous is all."

"Trust me. Trust us!" says Tom. "You're like, what? Almost forty?"

"Hey, hey," interrupts Neil. "I'm more like thirty-five... ish." They laugh.

"Yes, yes. But it's been, what? Five years since Tessa. You need this Neil. See what's out there."

"Yeah, I hear ya, thanks Tom."

"Anytime buddy. 'Kay, I gotta run. It's almost dinner time, and Louise'll kill me if I'm late."

"*Whhapshh!*" Neil snaps an imaginary whip.

"Yeah, yeah," says Tom.

"Ah, just kiddin' ya Tommy! Sounds nice."

They share a laugh.

Tom takes the steps down the deck to the driveway.

"Tomorrow night, 8 sharp, at The Smiling Lion! Be there or be square!" Tom jumps into his car and takes off down the driveway.

Neil cleans up some bottles and heads inside. He sits on the couch in his living room, picks up his issue of *The Wilmington News Journal* and the television remote. He flicks on the television and settles there at the coffee table. Neil looks at the front page and sets down the remote.

"Sara, at The Smiling Lion at 8 sharp," he whispers.

The next morning is clear and calm, like the day before. Neil's place on Purple Grape Road is teeming with life. Birds fly and play as a rabbit bounds down his driveway, making way for an orange S.U.V. Tom jumps out. He's wearing a gray jogging suit, white sneakers, and a white cap.

He seems quite awake and energetic for such an early morning visit. Neil calls out from the back deck before Tom can reach his front door.

"Mornin' buddy," says Tom.

"Top of the morning," replies Neil.

"Where you headed, all dressed up?" asks Neil sarcastically.

"It's comfy," says Tom, grabbing at his duds, as he trots toward Neil. "Louise says she may be able to get ya a place in town if you're interested. A real nice place too! A little smaller than this, but that's cool, right?"

"When did I ask y'all to find me a place to live?"

"I know, but this place here is in the middle of nowhere man. You ought to get closer to town, to civilization. Maybe find a new job even. Something that makes ya feel good."

"I'm good here Tom. I am. Tell Louise I'll pass this time, but thanks for lookin' out. Grab a coffee and have a seat, will ya?"

"No, no. I gotta get back. Had an hour to kill while Louise ran a few errands."

"Okay Tommy. Short and sweet!"

"Yeah buddy. Hey, y'know, if you aren't gonna move, you should at least get a phone. Would sure save on gas poppin' in on ya! How you ever gonna talk to Sara if you don't get connected? You're the only person in Delaware without one."

"Talk enough on the phone at work," replies Neil.

Tom laughs. "Have fun tonight, don't be late. Dinner's at eight!" he exclaims playfully.

Neil shakes his head and smiles as he walks inside.

Later that day, around 5 o'clock, after trying on about every shirt in his wardrobe, Neil stands in front of his bedroom mirror for a minute or two. He decides to drive down to the quaint little clothing shop he'd been known to frequent back when he felt a little better about things.

It's about twenty miles from his place in a miniature strip mall. Neil stares at himself for a moment before leaving. He is of average height and weight, has short, light brown hair, and is clean-shaven. He appreciates quality clothing and the importance of a freshly pressed shirt. *If I leave now, that's plenty of time to get here and get back to town to meet Sara*, he thinks to himself. Starting to feel like a rejuvenated man, with his new date approaching, Neil jumps in his black Chrysler and heads to the strip mall.

He pulls into the nearly empty lot and parks a few rows away from Supreme Tailor's Clothing Co. He does not notice two black Mercedes-Benz vans with no distinguishing differences pull in and drive to the row just behind his car.

After a brief encounter with a shirt rack and the young woman working the checkout, Neil comes out carrying a very nice, sheik, collared green shirt by its hanger.

He approaches his car, unlocks the door, and grabs a suit bag hanging from a single hook above his backseat side window. He carefully slides it over his new shirt, then pops his trunk lid from inside the car with a free hand.

Neil decides to lay the garment flat on his immaculate trunk floor. As he bends over to put it inside, the trunk lid comes crashing down on him. His shouts are muffled within the confined space as two men dressed head to toe in black sit on top of the trunk to pin him down. Another man, dressed identically, sticks his thigh with a syringe.

After a few seconds, the pain in his body subsides and Neil stops struggling. They quickly remove him from the trunk, carry him to the van and take off.

# 6
# Roebuck

The surface of Lake Utah, on the west side of the valley, looks like a mirror this morning. It captures and reflects the white-capped mountains perfectly. Up to the water's edge walks a large-statured man, of no more than forty years of age, Roebuck. His big shadow stretches far behind him, almost tripling him in length. He is of fair complexion, has short, blond curly hair and pale blue eyes. He wears denim coveralls, green rubber boots, and a Denver Broncos hat, which looks like it may have been orange at some point in the past, now sun-bleached and faded, it appears as a washed-out shade of pink.

Roebuck is on the grassy shoreline looking out at the endless mountainous landscape. The man looks at the upside-down crystal-clear reflection and then upward to the real thing. He clutches a small, gray tackle box in his left hand and a well-kept fishing rod in his right.

He is alone. In his deep tone of voice and drawn-out way of speaking, he says, "Well Daddy, I know we never had much luck to mention out here, but I feel I might catch us one today." Roe grins as he looks up at the clouds before kneeling down and rigging his line.

A half hour passes before his pole tugs ever so slightly. Roebuck raises his eyebrows and, without much effort, reels in a teeny tiny Crappie.

"Less than a pound," mumbles Roe. "Barely even ounces," he adds, as he gently frees the fish and guides it down into the lake. He fishes another hour or so and then packs up his tackle. Roe heads to his pickup truck.

His cellphone vibrates.

"Good morning, Roe the mover…! Uh, yes, that's right ma'am… Uh huh. Sounds like I could move you in one load actually… Yes, later today? My pleasure ma'am… Absolutely. When's the best for you? Okay Rosemary, I'll call you when I'm on my way. No. Thank *you*."

Dusk is settling on Salt Lake City with giant blankets of blue, pink, and orange. Roebuck and his helper bring the last two boxes into Rosemary's new apartment.

She stands at the doorway of the ground-level low-rise unit. "Thank you so much child."

"No problem," says Jim, a boy no older than seventeen. "I'll be in the cube van," he says to Roe as he heads toward it.

"And thank *you* Roe."

"Oh, no problem, Rosemary. Enjoy your new place." With a nod, he heads to join Jim at the van.

"I'm going to miss that lemonade!" he calls out before climbing up in.

A small bit of laughter comes from the elderly woman as she sees them off.

"Good stuff today, Jimmy. I don't know what I'd do without ya."

"Thanks Roe," says Jim proudly.

"You need to make any stops before I drop ya home?"

"Uh, no thanks. My mom's making meatloaf tonight. That's all I need right about now!"

"Can I come for dinner?" Roe asks with a wink.

"Don't know if there'd be enough for the likes 'o *you*," replies Jimmy.

"Now wait a minute! What are you implying?"

"Just that you're a great, big, giant!"

Roebuck laughs as if he's never heard anything like this before. Jimmy laughs too.

"Alright, alright, keep it all to yourself!" says Roe playfully.

Later that night, Roe passes the time logging his latest job into his record book and going over jobs of the recent past. His file cabinet is conveniently doubling as the end table beside his couch. It holds all his important files, as well as a lamp and a couple doilies his late grandmother had made him long ago.

The more he reads, the more tired he gets. The local news drones on across the television in front of him on low volume. The clock on the ticker at the bottom of the screen reads 10:50 p.m. Roe slowly packs up his things and puts them inside his cabinet. He chooses to sleep on the couch again tonight.

He sets the sleep timer on his T.V. to ninety minutes, then puts his cap on his face. It is about two hours later, Roe is fast asleep and snoring away, when four men, with masks on and dressed in all black, walk fast through the front lawn of his back-road dwelling. The kitchen is behind Roe, directly across the living room. A shine emits softly from a nightlight above the stove and reflects onto the brass knob on the inside of the door that leads directly outside. It slowly begins to turn. Big Roe, doesn't hear them coming. They surround him. He thrashes when two men simultaneously take hold of his arms and legs. A third covers his eyes and mouth with a rag and the fourth man renders him unconscious.

# 7
# Willy

'The Cacti Lounge' blinks in lime-green neon above a smaller sign in baby blue. It reads:

*'The place where Santa Fe comes to play.'*

Willy, looking very much like something the cat dragged in, walks up to the door puffing on a cigarette. The short, thin man looks no older than thirty-five. He has long hair, grown out to his chin. It is thick, dirty blond and is protruding from the sides and back of his weathered, soiled, yellow Pennzoil ball cap. His eyes are hazel, and his features are subtle. He could use a shave and a change of clothes would positively serve him but, he seems well-received, nonetheless.

"Hey dude!" says a much bigger man at the opened front doors. The two exchange pleasantries and shake hands.

The cover of Joni Mitchell's classic song '*Woodstock*'—by Crosby, Stills, Nash, and Young—can be heard there within the chatter as the blended reverberations emanate from the tavern and pass through the entrance way.

"Any sweeties tonight?" asks Willy.

"Not too bad," replies the big man.

"Cool. I'll catch up with ya inside." Willy flicks his smoke and heads in.

He walks through the bar. It is almost full to capacity. He receives plenty of shout-outs from patrons.

'Willy! Hey! How ya doin'?' and the like.

Willy is accepted by most, though he is an outsider.

The young man has had a hard life and an even harder upbringing.

He was forced to live with his abusive grandfather after his single mother up and disappeared one day. For years, he struggled in and out of various schools for 'failing to fall in line,' as most authority figures of the school board would agree, he simply just wouldn't apply himself.

During the time with his unforgiving grandfather, he resorted to running away. Breaking free from the abuse, he drifted all over New Mexico and even parts of Chihuahua until; only settling down within the last few years back in Santa Fe. He stayed on friends' couches and partook in a couple of failed relationships, until finally taking government assistance to pay for affordable housing on the edge of town.

It's not that he's lazy or hopeless. For Willy, it's quite the opposite. He's been chewed up and spit out far too often, and if given the proper chance and a little support, Willy could do well for himself. Willy, like many youths, has been dealt a bad hand.

He is a man, like far too many men and women, who seems to always have the worst of luck in a world that can often be so cold. First his family had neglected him, then society had done the same.

Willy is only popular around town for being 'that guy.' The one you see throughout the community, the one who is always outgoing and even a little eccentric, almost manic. No one knows where he came from, where he lives, or where he's going. No one really cares. He shows up, entertains, and disappears. One thing Willy has always possessed, however, is endurance. He understands that people in his position must always focus on brighter days ahead. He makes his way through the long, dimly lit club. There is a bar to his left, a row of tables parallel to his right, and booths parallel to those. He finds a gap between two people at the bar and catches the bartender's attention. He motions to the beer on ice in a steel trough opposite the counter. Upon purchasing one, he twists the lid off his bottle and turns around just in time to notice a large, big-bellied man in his late fifties stride by holding a pint of his own.

"Hey! Bruce!" calls Willy to the older man; he looks big and burly in an outfit resembling work clothes, but they are far too clean to have actually been put through anything. Bruce stops.

"Hey Buck," he says.

"What about some work for me?" inquires Willy.

"Ah, you don't want it," returns Bruce.

"You know I do! I been askin' ya every time I see ya, every chance I get."

"Oh, I know Buck, I know."

"Look, you got a great building company. One of the biggest from here to Albuquerque. Why won't you plug me in somewhere on one of your jobsites? I'll do anything, man! Put me on a shovel, I don't care! I'll live attached to a wheelbarrel," urges Willy desperately. "What have you got to lose?"

"I'm goin' back to my booth boy, you catch up with me there," says Bruce.

"Yeah, sure, okay," replies Willy. For the moment, his fervor wanes.

Big Bruce blends into the crowd.

"Do you believe that guy?" says Willy to the pretty blonde beside him.

"Uh, I dunno," says the tipsy woman. She is oblivious.

Willy smiles and takes the long way around the bar to find Bruce's booth. He receives the odd shouts of almost-condescending sounding greetings. The kind that make you wonder if Willy is even liked at all by the people calling to him; he smiles, though, and shouts back all the same. The large man is sitting with his wife—Jill, a younger gold-digging type, so goes the rumor—and an employee that Willy recognizes from one of the work sites he had scouted.

"Ah, jeez," mumbles Bruce as he motions his worker to move down the seat to let Willy in. Jill begins to groan.

"Hi Buck," says Bruce with a wry smile. "That's Tyler. He's new."

"Taylor," says Taylor.

Bruce seems to not hear him.

"And you know Jill."

"Yep," says Willy as she gives a miserable, forced smirk.

"So, Bruce, what would be so terrible about giving me a job? I have lots of experience."

"We're good Bucko," says Bruce arrogantly.

"You hire and fire guys all the time!" Taylor's eyes widen, just for a second upon hearing Willy's claim.

"So why not just gimme a try, even for a day. I won't disappoint. I'm a keeper, you'll see!"

"No," says Bruce with conviction.

"Look mister, I need money... Everyone needs money. I've done construction, and I'm seasoned in hard manual labor. I look for a job everywhere I go with no resolve. What gives? I can't make heads or tails of it. You're a man who could help me, even part-time would help me."

The four stare across the table at one another for a moment, until Bruce begins to laugh. A young woman from the table to the left and directly across from theirs had quite obviously been eavesdropping, and she too appears to be interested in what Bruce might say next.

"Get the fuck outta here!" snaps Jill sharply. Taylor jumps. She sips her strawberry daiquiri and glares at Willy.

"What the hell!" he says in utter shock.

"Just go! You…dirty little scrub," she says.

Bruce, now belting out a thunderous laughter, manages to mutter a suggestion, "Now, now Jilly. Let's control ourselves honey."

"No Bruce!" shouts Jill. "This little prick bothers you every time he sees you. Enough is enough!"

Taylor searches both men's faces, as if hanging by the moment.

"Hey, screw you! You ignorant little bitch!" shouts the young woman who's been closely following the escalating conversation from the table across the way. "And you too! You fat jerk," she adds as she shoots a look of disgust at Bruce.

"And just who the fuck are *you?* Slut!" exclaims Jill, clearly flush from her booze buzz.

"I'm the silent majority," yells the young woman as she rises and stands beside the booth.

She grabs Willy's shoulder.

"You filthy creeps! This poor guy is asking you for probationary employment so he can get by, maybe earn a shot at a living, and you spit in his face! SHAME ON YOU!" she shouts.

Willy is stunned as he watches his surprise ally ambush the scene.

"Let's go Willy," orders the woman. She yanks him from the booth by his arm and pulls him through the bar by the cuff of his shirtsleeve and out front to the sidewalk.

"Um… Thanks! Who are you?" asks Willy. He is bewildered.

"I'm Juliette."

"Why did you do that for me, Juliette?"

"You don't remember me, do you?"

"No, should I?"

"Yes!" she shouts. "Juliette from Chilliwack Middle School!"

"Uh, nope," replies Willy as he explores his memory bank.

"Well, you were only there for a few months. Grade six, right?"

"Uh-huh, less than that." Willy is still confused by what's happening.

"I was the girl who got stuck on the monkey bars?" she says as if asking a question.

"And?" says Willy, provoking her to elaborate.

"One recess, I was all alone playing on them. I hooked my legs on either sides of the top rungs and hung upside down. I got stuck, I couldn't pull myself back upright; I was too weak, I guess. My legs were bruising, and I was terrified that I was gonna fall and break my neck. It felt like forever! Soon, a crowd of kids gathered. I screamed while they pointed and laughed at me. I'm pretty sure the whole school was there. I was mortified." Juliette pauses a moment. "That's when you came. You pushed your way through everyone and climbed up to me. You told me it was okay, that I'd be fine. You helped me up and freed my legs. You scolded everyone; you told them they were mean and awful. The crowd left. You said 'forget 'em' and told me not to worry cause I was safe. You took me to the classroom to our teacher Mrs. Sullivan and went back outside. I never thanked you." Juliette smiles. "You stopped attending shortly after."

"I don't remember," says Willy.

"It was you, I know it was you," she says firmly.

"Well Miss Juliette, I thank you right back!"

"Anytime, Willy." She smiles again. "I gotta head home. Most of my girlfriends have gone back there already, and they've had more to drink than I can stand tonight; they've probably puked all over my place by now."

"Hello! You stupid bitch!" screams one of her friends, who is particularly lacking some important motor skills, as she approaches.

"Have a safe trip home, Juliette. Thanks for sticking up for me."

The clumsy girls lock arms and proceed walking energetically down the sidewalk.

Juliette twists back around and shouts, "Hey, Willy!"

"Yeah?" he calls.

"Forget 'em!" She then turns and continues to strut into the shadows of the night.

Feeling slightly bitter-sweet, Willy lights up a cigarette. Bruce lumbers through the front doors with his entourage.

"Hey! It's Buck," he calls out while a few random smokers look on.

"Ah, FUCK YOU BRUCE! It's Willy, you son of a bitch! My name is Willy and you know it."

"What's the difference?" mumbles Bruce. "Jill thinks that you're embarrassing," he adds. "Your appearance, your hygiene, and your personality. We think you'd be bad for the company's image. Like uh…" Bruce searches for a euphemism, "a black mark… or a stain!" he shouts while raising his index finger to the air.

"You ignorant son of a bitch," says Willy in a calm, collected tone. He sniffs and looks Bruce dead in the eyes. "Go fuck yourself," he adds, before walking away along the sidewalk.

A few blocks down from the Cacti club. Willy ducks into the first alley he finds and discovers two black Mercedes vans parked in a row, facing opposite him, with five men in all black clothing standing at the lead vehicle. Its hood is propped open. One man is talking on a cellphone. They notice Willy and immediately appear alarmed. The man on the phone quickly hangs up as the others scramble in front of the engine and fumble with some tools. As Willy approaches and walks alongside the vans, he calls out, "Problem friends? Y'all okay?" he asks, as he arrives closer. The group of men and their appearance become clear.

"Geez, I ain't never seen you guys 'round here," he says, now standing amongst all five men at the front of the van. "What's with the ski masks…y'all fixin' to rob a bank? I'm in," he says with a laugh as one of the more under-prepared men quickly pulls his mask down over his exposed face. Willy does not notice a sixth man come up behind him from the shadows.

"Hey Willy!" he shouts. The man takes out a black forty-caliber silenced handgun from his sweater pouch.

"How'd you know my—" Just then the man smashes Willy in the face with the side of the pistol, his hat goes flying from the impact and he falls to the ground.

"What the fuck!" yells Willy. He springs to his feet as quickly as he was knocked off them. "You done did it now!" he shouts. He clenches his fist and connects a right cross with the man who struck him. His adversary falls hard onto his rear-end. Willy punches and kicks in defense at all the encroaching men.

He holds his own as they shuffle and struggle with the quick and wiry fight he puts up. After a minute, the side door of the van slowly slides open and two more men dressed in all-black clothing step out. One is gripping a rusted tire iron. The man walks calmly into the commotion and situates himself behind Willy. He steadily takes aim. His first down stroke proves to be his last. The tire iron catches the ever-feisty Willy on the top of his head and sends a split down the front center of his forehead. This time, he is knocked down and stays there. The group stare down at Willy from the circle they have formed.

"There'll be no need to administer the keto-benzo needle right now," says the man with the tire-iron callously.

"Nor the chloroform blend, either," adds another man.

The group collects Willy's limp body and his bloodied Pennzoil hat. They throw him into the nearest van. The driver of the lead vehicle closes its hood. The eight men divide into two groups of four and the pair of vans exit the alley.

# 8

# Into the Wilderness

Dawn breaks and the sun saturates the vast horizon of tall trees, shining brightly onto a massive forest, highlighting the endless green wilderness and blazing through its treetops. Giant streaks of cloud smear distant parts of the sky in an otherwise clear blue morning. The woods are alive with wildlife. Countless species carry about with their sounds and calls, from every angle within the thicket, as the diurnal animals wake to grant the nocturnal dwellers of the forest their leave.

Two blue jays flutter and flap their wings. They dance and play, weaving in between and all around the treetops. The tips swing and sway with a life force of their own below the blue birds.

Where the trees meet the sky, the vegetation is dense. It's the surface of a world hiding infinite complexities beneath it.

The blue jays land on a treetop together but stay only briefly. They disperse, giving way to a large bald eagle. It glides into view and freefalls to a tip of his own, landing effortlessly. The eagle rocks back and forth upon it. Before long, the tree is still. The glorious bird looks far off into the distance from his perch. The world is his... After a few moments, with its golden eyes, the eagle looks down into the forest.

At ground level, a narrow creek winds about twenty yards down at the bottom of an incline from a small, dilapidated shack. It steadily flows along and pours into a heavily wooded and particularly rocky stretch of nearby terrain.

The sun's rays penetrate through the branches and leaves from above, they cause the rushing water to shimmer in spots and cast a bright glare onto the weathered, galvanized steel that sheets the element-beaten structure. The one-room building is two hundred and fifty square feet at best. It appears long forgotten and stands slouched and crooked with a corner sunken into the earth.

Tall grass and bushes surround most of it tightly. Its gray barn boards are decrepit, with open knotholes throughout and deep splits between its grains.

If a door had ever been installed at all, it is missing. A baby rabbit bounds from around the corner of the sad, old shack and sniffs the doorframe and then pushes its nose inside before abruptly hopping away. Further inside the shack, near the immediate right corner, is a long side table with a single drawer. A dense layer of dirt lay caked on its surface.

It is warped and twisted way out of its original square.

The wooden floor is damaged with gouges throughout. In the far corner down from the table, a burlap sack lays there in tatters. On top of the shreds is a pile of well-manicured synthetic material, it is fluffed up, just so with a sizeable indent in its center.

On the other side of the shack are two single beds. They are set closely, side by side, the mattress on the right has a large hole in its side and is heavily stained. On top lays a man…Charlie.

Between the two parallel set beds, sits a small, two-tier end table with both drawers missing. The piece of furniture is just as damaged and distorted as the one across from it by the door. On the even dirtier bed on the left lay Simon.

A strip of sunlight runs down his face and chest through a narrow gap in the roof sheeting above. On the edge of the void, between the tarnished steel and moist, rotten lumber, a small amount of water has welled up from the morning's condensation. It begins to vibrate, as the hollow of the crevice cannot collect and hold any more run-off from the topside. Finally, some dew breaks free to allow for more water.

Gravity accepts the excess, and a single droplet falls to Simon's forehead.

The first drop goes unnoticed, and the second does too, until a small stream splashes onto his brow. It runs past the inside of his eye and along his cheek, some finds rest in the corner of his closed mouth, while the rest rolls off his chin. Simon slowly rubs his lips and his eyes. He winces and opens them. After several blinks, he stares up through the gap in the ceiling and out to the towering tree branches above.

He hears birds chirping beyond the roof, and as his mind begins to collect parts of his reality, he furrows his brow and struggles to sit up. Simon leans his back against the wall behind him. He studies the side table by the door, peers outside with a squint, and then rubs his eyes again. He begins to search his suit with subtle pats on each pocket, one by one, until he finds his glasses. With another furrow of his brow, he puts them on. Both lenses are broken. Simon is incredibly confused. He takes his useless glasses off and lays them carefully on the mattress.

He spots Charlie in the next bed. With an instinctual jolt, he springs to his feet. Simon holds his breath and covers his mouth firmly. He is wide-eyed and slowly backs toward the doorway. He turns and stumbles outside to find a bright green, lush world. He spins back around and looks at the shack. He pats himself down again in search of his cellphone, but it is gone, along with his wallet. Simon's anxieties intensify. "What is happening?" he whispers to himself. His head is pounding.

He quickly scans the surrounding forest...up and down, side to side and all over. Simon does his best to push aside the terror and tries to remember how he got there. For a few moments, he is blank, until finally he gasps. He remembers work, the old lady, lunch at The Spot, and the parking garage.

Simon recalls being struck and then succumbing to the darkness. He runs back into the building and reaches Charlie. He stops short and analyses him as he sleeps. He looks around for something, anything! He darts back outside and picks up the first rock he sees, one that's big enough to use effectively yet small enough to hold in one hand.

He enters the shack a third time and carefully approaches Charlie. "HEY!" he yells. Nothing happens.

"HEY!" again, nothing…

He puts his left foot on the mattress, braces against the floor with his right and proceeds to shake the bed with great force.

Charlie wakes relatively quickly.

"Whoa! Whoa! Whoa!" shouts Charlie as he puts his hands up and looks around shocked.

"Who the hell are you?" yells Simon.

"What? I'm Charlie! I'm Charlie! Who are you?" he urges.

"Why are you here?" questions Simon, in a menacing tone of voice.

"Uh… Where? I don't know!" yells Charlie as he looks all over.

"I am Simon! Now, *who* are you? And where am I?" he demands.

"Simon, I don't know who *you* are *or* where I am! I swear to you!" begs Charlie.

Simon searches Charlie's face. The man is as scared and confused as he is. He drops the rock, and his eyes soften. He nods to the door.

"Go see," he says, now with a calm, collected demeanor.

Charlie gets up with arms lower by his side but palms still facing Simon; he walks outside and turns three-hundred-and-sixty degrees to best observe the woods.

"Simon, what's going on?"

"I don't know. I woke up here too. I'm sorry, but I thought…"

"It's okay," says Charlie.

"Where the hell are we?"

Charlie, still scanning his surroundings, begins, "I was in my backyard…watching the birds…I remember… A very sharp pain," he says in a way one would when trying to sort out a dream.

Charlie rubs his head to find a large bump.

"Same here," adds Simon.

"I was assaulted in the parking garage where I work… I think I was hit on the head. That's all I remember. Feels like a long time ago."

A determination comes over Charlie as he looks Simon in the eyes. "We have got to get out of here."

"You're goddamn right we do."

"This can't be Tampa," says Charlie.

"Why would we be in Tampa?" snaps Simon loudly.

"It's where I'm from, where I live… Simon, where are *you* from?" asks Charlie, afraid of what he might hear.

"Seattle," answers Simon, appearing bewildered.

The two men look at each other, not knowing what to make of the situation.

Seconds feel like minutes as they pass.

"We're prisoners, we're prisoners here," Charlie speaks up as he repeats it.

"But why?" asks Simon.

"I don't know…but we have got to get out of here!" exclaims Charlie. "We need to get away from the forest and into civilization. We can figure it out then—"

"Just hold on Charlie, just wait."

"For what? Simon! We've got to get moving!"

"Which way?"

"I'm going to search the shed quickly, maybe I'll find… something useful. Anything! Then, we can figure which way to head out," answers Charlie.

"Okay…alright, while you're doing that," Simon points down toward the incline, "I'm going to take a drink from the creek. I'm about to fucking die."

"Yes, yes, but hurry!"

Charlie turns and disappears into the shack as Simon runs down toward the water.

Charlie opens the long, side table drawer. He rummages through the burlap sack, examines inside the end table with no drawers, shoves his hand inside the hole in the mattress, and then proceeds to flip them both over. He doesn't find a thing. In frustration, he tosses the end table and pulls the side table over onto it's face in the hopes that there is something to be found underneath the pieces of furniture. There is not.

At the narrow creek, Simon is at the water's edge. The atmosphere is eerily calm and quiet, as the two men have likely succeeded in scaring off just about every living creature within a mile radius. The only sound is that of the running water before him.

From his knees, he fills his cupped hands with the cold, crystal-clear water.

After a few moments of eagerly refreshing himself Simon hears a noise and stops what he is doing. He tilts his head, raises his ear to the air and keeps himself still. A second later, a loud bang rips through the woods. A bullet slips into Simon's temple and out the other side, blood leaps out of his head and follows the bullet's exit. The echo from the shot reverberates and bounces off the trees within the forest. Simon slumps sideways and falls into the creek, face first with a splash. The water instantly changes from clear to crimson.

The red cloud continues to envelope the creek as the water and blood mix together and flow down current, the same direction Simon has fallen.

Charlie jumps to the doorway of the shack where he can get a brief glimpse of Simon. He observes his lifeless body in the water. Charlie's mind reels. He can't deduce exactly where the shot had come from, considering the series of echoes that had sounded off, but quickly determines that it likely had come from his and Simon's left given to the trajectory in which Simon's dead body lay slumped awkwardly to the right side.

With his adrenaline pumping and not another second to lose, Charlie, takes off in the opposite direction of the shooter's most probable vantage point. He runs faster than he ever has in his entire life as he vanishes deeper into the forest.

# 9

# Not Alone

The woods are robust and thriving. Cascading shades of green pour out from every part of the vast landscape with a grand radiance. Strewn about the immediate vicinity and towering gigantically above are magnificent arrays of maple, ash, birch, and oak trees. There are several types of bushes and many species of plants filling the voids and making up the forest floor.

A large cluster of boulders rest at the base of a cliff that edges and divides the earth as far as Charlie can see along either side of it. Down below amongst thick bushes and intertwining vines, he sits with his legs bent at the knees and squeezed together in front of himself; he clutches around his shins with his arms locked at his hands. Charlie is set and hidden just so, in a space between the massive rocks. A large, thick mat of moss spills over the boulders. The layer of overgrowth makes up the small perforation's roof and hangs over the front of its opening. It seems to Charlie that if he sits there long enough, the giant, off-balance fragment of moss just might release itself and flop to the ground in front of him. He's certain it wouldn't happen that way, that such a healthy, developed patch of moss would first have to dry out considerably and die before it would detach in such a setting, if at all. He imagines it happening anyway and fantasizes about it trapping him there inside his small hiding place.

The distraught man is dirty and has scrapes and cuts on his arms and face. He appears to be gaunt as he looks out into the green oblivion. Charlie is clearly shaken by the latest turn of events. As he stares off, he remembers Simon and the shack and his last hours at home in Tampa. Nothing makes sense. Charlie wonders why he is in this foreign place. He is not 'in bad' with anyone he knows. Charlie wonders if anybody else is out here. If there are any more people hiding in the brush.

He wonders…if he finds anyone, how could he trust them after that? He will know, he supposes. Just as poor Simon knew to trust *him*. Hours pass as Charlie watches the forest before him and listens for any sounds that could be significant to his dilemma.

Morning turns to afternoon, and he has been telling himself that sooner or later, he must move. He must try to get out and that staying still and hidden may preserve his safety only in the short-term, it likely won't be a positive long-term solution. Eventually, if he doesn't starve to death, some kind of animal might get him while he's still alive, a bear, a cougar, a pack of wolves perhaps. Charlie shakes such negative thoughts from his mind and musters the necessary courage to move forward, but before he sets out, he needs to verify the direction in which he will trek. He decides to continue following the same way he had ran, before he jumped off the mossy hill and discovered his current hiding spot.

He knows the shooter could be anywhere by now, but to keep in the same direction he had gone, he feels, is his best option. Ideally, he'd have surely considered following the flow of the creek in one direction or the other, but it's counter-productive to dwell on what could have been. Besides, he just might meet up with it or another one at some point.

Charlie walks through the forest slowly stepping over shrubs and rock. His feet still damp from the mornings run through wet grass. He weaves through the wild, ducking low-laying branches and never straying too far from the clearest path, he hopes will lead him to civilization.

The hours roll on, with Charlie often halting at the various sounds of the forest. He decides to take a rest in a hollow he finds within a cluster of thorn bushes. He is out of sight and hopes the thorns can protect him from bigger animals, but still remains fearful. The frustration of his predicament always prevalent and on his mind.

*Could this be Washington?* He wonders as he sits studying a large maple tree.

He knows he is not in Tampa Bay. Charlie lowers his head to his hands at another thought of Simon and how his life came to such a sudden and horrifically tragic end. He thinks of how helpless he is feeling. Slowly, he lays down on the ground, within the thorns. He proceeds to search his mind, to try to recollect anything at all that could have him arriving at this place.

Why is he here…? He comes up blank with absolutely no hypothesis. His reality amazes him in the worst of ways.

Birds begin to chirp again all around him. He hears a woodpecker off in the distance.

*How at ease*, he thinks to himself, *that bird is completely in its element, simply hammering away with not a care in the world.*

The trees above sway ever so slightly; Charlie observes the clouds drifting by above in the darkening sky.

He is exhausted, so he falls into a deep slumber.

Dusk passes over the woods, and as the Sun begins to set into the trees, the only sound is that of a man trudging through the forest.

Neil walks at a fast, determined pace, he seems to have the same idea Charlie had earlier.

With night quickly approaching, he clambers faster and faster with every step. The wilderness is getting the better of him. He too must stop to rest or even sleep. Frustrated, he looks around at the surrounding area to find a good place to lay. Neil, as is Charlie and as was Simon, is extremely confused by his predicament.

Neil figures he is alone. He hadn't heard the shot, as he was still asleep when it occurred. He didn't wake up in *his* shack with company either. He is even more perplexed by his reality. But Neil does know a few fundamental truths, he knows he was taken and that he must get out of the forest. Although, for now, he needs to rest, if he can. Neil had walked most of the day.

He chooses an area beneath a tree and lies still, assuring himself it will all be okay. After futile ruminations, the fatigue overcomes him, and he too is asleep.

Stars are embedded like diamonds in the night sky. The first-quarter moon shines brightly, casting a luminous white glow on the clearer areas of the forest below.

Across the woods, Charlie wakes up fast and jumps to his feet. His grogginess quickly replaced by adrenaline. Near and far are the noises of coyote's as they howl and carry on. *Sounds like…witches screaming out*, he whispers. He does his best to keep his wits about him. Despite the disturbing sounds, he remains as composed as he can, before carefully leaving the thorn maze in a very slow and calculated manner. There are more eerie sounds. *They sound like adolescent laughter and crying babies*, he thinks. Charlie shakes the thought from his head. Under the cover of darkness, he believes he can make good ground on whoever is out there, just as long as he is careful walking and ignores the sounds and scenarios that provoke his imagination to wander off to the macabre.

Moonlight is prominent enough to allow him to maneuver decently. He slowly but surely advances through the forest, all while doing his best to effectively block out all the strange animal noises nightfall has brought with it. They come in and out, all over the untamed woods. Charlie walks well, picking up his pace through the hours, repetitively stopping in the hopes of eyeing any man-made light through the thickness of his surroundings. As he goes, he wonders what day and time it is. It dawns on him that the *time* depends on where in the world he has been taken to. The thought of this makes him feel even more lost. He thinks of all the species of insect, amphibian, and wild animal that are surely lurking and instantly changes his thoughts to more positive ones. He speed-walks to a hopeless jog and eventually finds himself scrambling in an area of the forest much more rugged than before.

Visibility hits an all-time low, as a massive cloud swallows the moon and the brush seems to be closing in and swallowing Charlie up too. As the moonlight fades, he is extremely frustrated and fights the grip of the bushes as they grab and tug at his clothing as if to purposely hold him. He imagines the branches of the thorn bushes turn into long, pointed, crooked fingers on fractured hands attached to disjointed arms. They continuously close in with their tight, unrelenting grasps and cut him all over. He struggles mightily. It seems that he has worked his way into a position where he is fully and completely surrounded by thorn bushes. He quits the battle and unleashes a disturbing yell from the pit of his empty stomach. Charlie bows his head in defeat. Moments pass slowly.

"Oh, Mom," he says aloud… Then, he whispers, "I'm scared. I'm so, so scared," he admits to the thin air. His breath is slightly visible in the cooler temperature.

Charlie soon grows angry and starts to thrash his body about in attempt to break free from the bushes. Suddenly, he does, and his momentum flings him forward, forcing him to take a few running steps through the thicket until he falls about ten feet down a hill, over rocks, and through more thorns. He hits the ground below and lands hard. Charlie pulls himself together into a seated position. A pack of animals sound off again from nearby. He painstakingly takes his shirt off. Now shivering, he rolls his shirt lengthwise and ties it tight around his head, covering his eyes and ears.

The next morning, weather-wise, it is no different than the last. Sunshine and clear skies give way to a robust place, teeming with wildlife. Neil is walking with purpose again and reminisces about the last day. The one before he woke up lost. He is grateful that nighttime is behind him. He thinks about Tommy and Louise but mostly about the Smiling Lion and the girl he never met…Sara. He thinks about how silly it was that he would have ever been nervous about such a great opportunity. He laments on how odd it is to try and picture a person he has never seen and tries to imagine her despite how minimal a description of her he had gotten.

She is probably beautiful, he affirms. He was so laxed about meeting her when he was home, he recalls. *I can't wait to get back and reach out to her,* thinks Neil. He even misses the call-center and the people he would talk to and daydreams about his life left behind while navigating through the obstacles of the hostile terrain. He snaps out of it when he sees something too important to overlook. Something about a hundred yards through the trees and in a clearing. He can hardly make it out visually, other than that it appears black, is of decent size, and is of an interesting shape. Anything that is unusual within the forest that can be helpful in any way is definitely worth investigating. Breaking his chosen course, Neil turns toward the foreign object.

Charlie wakes to the infamous chirping of birds. More woodland noises that are all-too-familiar to him by now. He removes his makeshift blindfold and earmuffs to see a substantially clearer stretch of land that is much less dense than the area ten feet above and behind him. He rubs his eyes feeling indifferent about the morning before him. On one hand, he can walk better in daylight, but on the other, so can Simon's killer, if in fact he is still around. Charlie hopes that he isn't but cannot imagine his abduction and Simon's murderer not being connected. As he begins to focus on the landscape before him, he notices an old carriage or wagon off in the distance, he is uncertain which.

He gets up slowly and begins to walk toward it. As he gets close, the object reveals itself.

"A rickshaw," he whispers. "How would *you* have gotten out here?" he asks while rubbing the lump on his head. He recalls the curious little flag in his backyard and what he had asked of *it*.

The vehicle, only about forty feet away now as he approaches, is very old and weathered but must have been impressive in its day. It is black and blue, with faded golden trim lines here and there, and has burgundy French provincial style leather upholstery. The material is dried out and cracked allover.

It's complete, with a pair of large wheels with wooden spokes. They are sunken many inches into the ground. The land nearby is particularly wet, there are several puddles within the grass. Charlie, extremely parched, bends down for a drink, vigorously cupping the water to his chapped lips, before resuming toward the antique vehicle. "Hellooo!" shouts a man to Charlie's distant left. He spins around quick to see someone about fifty yards away jogging toward him within the wide-open space. Charlie abandons his defensive stance when the man gets closer. He notices that the guy is almost as dirty and scratched up as he is and most importantly unarmed, so much as he can tell.

"Hello!" calls the man again as he gains ground. Charlie looks as if he's staring at a ghost.

"Hey… I'm Charlie," he says in a quiet voice upon the man's arrival.

"Who are you?" he asks.

"Hello Charlie, I'm Neil."

# 10

# Insight

"How did you get here?" whispers Charlie.

"I don't know. It's messed up... A complete nightmare. I woke up in some shed, and I've been on foot since yesterday," replies Neil. "You as well? By the look of you, am I right, Charlie?"

"Yes, except I was not alone. There was another with me."

Neil studies Charlie's face.

"Simon was his name... Shortly after we woke, he was shot in the head from long range. We didn't see it coming and I didn't see the shooter," Charlie says, as if in shame.

"What? Oh, my God!" exclaims Neil.

"Do you remember being taken?" asks Charlie.

"I remember getting fucked up at my car by some men. I didn't see them. I was ambushed... I passed out."

"I don't even know how long ago that was," says Neil, appearing defeated as he looks to the ground. He continues... "I figured I was dumped here, maybe for the car, maybe they were tracking me...robbed my house."

"No, this is something much bigger...we're prisoners," proclaims Charlie. A moment passes while Charlie looks off into the distance. "You didn't hear the shot?"

"No," answers Neil.

"Tell me, where are you from?"

"Delaware."

Charlie shakes his head.

"Why?" urges Neil. "You?"

"Tampa."

"What?"

"I know," Charlie concurs with Neil's shocked reaction and can certainly relate. "Listen Neil, I'm not sure of anything here. Are you a person of importance or anything like that?"

"Well, I'd like to hope so, but not in the way you're insinuating…! Why? Are you?"

"No, I'm a struggling writer of sorts," answers Charlie. "I've almost finished my first book." He manages a grin, "It's a fictitious story about a group of men amidst a mystery."

"I work at a crisis call center," says Neil.

"Man, they took my wallet, my—"

"Listen!" interrupts Charlie. "We were snatched up and brought here to who-knows-where. The first guy I met here was murdered. There are two things we need to do."

"What are they?" asks Neil.

"One…get the hell out of this God-forsaken forest…and two…don't get killed on our way."

"Charlie, if you woke with someone else, and here I am, there might be more of us out here. Guys just like us trying to figure this fucked-up situation out, and if so, we need to find them!"

"I have thought of that too, Neil, but if we find anybody else, we need to find them on our way out. I am telling you, we cannot do circles in this place!"

"We can try to figure it all out later, when we're safe." Charlie stares right into Neil's eyes. "My friend, Simon didn't even see it coming."

"Okay, Charlie… Okay," agrees Neil.

"Which way should we go?"

Charlie points down past the rickshaw into the green abyss. "I've been heading that way. I've yet to completely witness the sunrise, but I *think* that way is south."

"South it is then, Charlie. That's pretty close to the direction I've been heading too."

The newly united duo takes up their chosen route. Neil stops, turns, and jogs back to the rickshaw. He grabs a wheel spoke and breaks it loose, then another, both are about eighteen inches long and very sharp on both ends. He meets back up with Charlie and hands him one.

"Better than nothing," he suggests. "Until we can upgrade."

The two men holster their newly acquired weapons in their belts. Neil down the small of his back and Charlie at his front-side and tilted diagonally toward his hip.

Time passes as the two steadily walk the woods with care. They slow down now and then to search for anything there is to find that could be helpful and after every unusual noise they hear. It is a beautiful and interesting place within the woods. If only they were there under different circumstances. Eventually, they are stopped at a small pond and proceed to drink.

"Best swamp water I've ever drunk," Neil says with a wink.

Charlie cannot muster the enthusiasm to laugh or even smile.

Though Neil has had it rough himself, it is obvious that what Charlie had witnessed before kept him distant and hardened.

"Well, it's apparent that whoever brought us here doesn't want us to know the exact time. I was wearing a nice watch."

Neil adds, looking at his wrist in the water's reflection. Charlie stops drinking and splashes his face.

"He's toying with us," says Charlie. Neil looks to him, and he continues, "Whoever is out there, and maybe there are several. But whatever is going on, it's possible we're being hunted." says Charlie with conviction. He stares down at his own wobbly reflection.

Neil does too. The men's faces are distorted as they agitate within the naturally occurring mirror.

"The person who murdered Simon...could be looking at us right now." Charlie watches his face slowly but surely become clearer. "Let's get out of here," he says.

They continue on, maintaining their instinctual strategy as they go. Obviously feeding off of each other's motivation, they are much more absorbed within the forest together than they were when they were alone. When the pair are not ducking for cover or scanning the landscape, the men gently and quietly speak of their past, of the life left behind, of loved ones and simple pleasures. Through the forest, the two eventually reach something that they both have to assure each other is not an apparition.

What Charlie and Neil have found is a Montmorency Cherry tree. Despite their better judgment, they cannot help but to shout their excitement and run to the fully grown, twenty-foot wide, twenty-foot tall fruit tree with great uninhibited vigor.

"*You're a sight for sore eyes,*" Charlie whispers to the tree as he catches his breath and reaches up through its bright white flowers and to a shiny, red morsel from underneath. A flock of Cedar Wax-wings fly off and leave the cherries to the newest visitors. The two mingle below. They pick and eat, merrily and for the time being, have forgotten all about the true reality of their awful situation, as if it were planned to meet under the cherry tree enjoy themselves and eat to their hearts' content. When finished, they lay out underneath the tree with red lips and full stomachs. The fruit revitalizing their systems. They gaze up and through the magnificent work of art that is the cherry tree and to the beautiful summer sky.

They laugh and tell jokes until, before long and without protest, they both surrender to a much-needed nap. For the moment, all is peaceful.

Charlie wakes about an hour later and nudges Neil.

They pick some more cherries, stuff their pockets with them, and continue onward.

After a while, they reach a heavily wooded and particularly bushy area. They come out of the thickness of the forestry to a sparse part of the woods. A place where, as far as the eye can see, there are wetlands. The men are stunned. There isn't any sign of potential civilization anywhere. Only vast marshland.

"There's too much of it," says Neil. "We would never make it through. It would take weeks to pass here…months, and to what end?" he adds.

"We've gotta turn back," says Charlie in disbelief. "*We've gotta turn back,*" he whispers. With motivation dwindled down, the two men head back the way they came. They are distraught.

They walk a few hours to where they are forced to climb a cliff. They help each other when necessary and make good time going up. It is about thirty feet to higher ground and is very steep and thick most of the way.

When they finally arrive at the top, Neil leans with his back to a giant oak tree. Charlie bends down to clear his shoe of twigs and dirt.

"Hey Charlie, there's a lot of pine and spruce. I think that's even Ontario Poplar," he says as he nods forward. Charlie puts his shoe back on as he looks down the way.

"What are you saying Neil? We're north, somewhere north?" he repeats.

"We've got to be," he replies.

Charlie looks wayward to the patch of pines. He spots a shiny, royal blue stretch of material amongst the trees. It looks like velvet or satin and in far too good of a condition to just have been hung out in the wilderness and left there. Charlie squints his eyes and observes that it is a cape lined with gold. As they focus more acutely, he sees a royal blue sash draped diagonally over the front of an elaborate matching tunic with a red collar.

At the bottom of the sash, there is a hilted, gold sword handle protruding from its sheath. Charlie is in a haze. Finally, he searches upward again and discovers that coming out from both sides of the cape are a man's outstretched arms and white-gloved hands, lined with red sleeve-cuffs, holding a golden rifle. The man is looking down its sights and pointing the gun right at them. Charlie's eyes pop open and fill with terror, as they catch up with the blurry mustached face directly behind the barrel.

"Look out!" he screams as the front end of the rifle lights up for a split-second with a flash. Neil is struck in the center of his chest and falls to his knees, staring wide-eyed into the distant woods.

His hands are covered in blood as he grabs and digs at the devastating wound. Then, with a second bang, Neil's stomach explodes, and he falls forward.

Once again powerless and fleeing for his life, Charlie runs a short distance and jumps high and far, throwing himself wildly off the edge of the cliff that he and Neil had just climbed so meticulously. He free-falls all the way down, through tree branches and along jagged rocks. He crashes at the bottom with a forceful impact.

He is majorly injured but manages to drag his body to a nearby Juniper bush, where he pushes himself underneath it's base with all his might.

Charlie remains still, wheezing as steadily and silently as possible.

# 11
# Recourse

The late afternoon had clouded over, and the air got heavy. When the wind kicks up, the trees start to sway and the leaves above another dilapidated shack begin to rustle, while long, hanging branches gently grind eerily along it's steel roof, over and back again. This structure is furnished inside with a single bed and a wardrobe housing a pair of books that have more than aged under the elements and in their neglect. An old corn broom that has had the life swept out of it decades ago is set in the corner, by the doorway.

Twenty yards down from the shack at a small clearing, a doe steps out of the thicket. As she does, snaps sound off on the ground as the animal steps through twigs and plants. Behind the forgotten building, a man is quietly and repetitively bending a large rectangle steel sheet back and forth at one of its corners. He stops quickly when he hears the snaps and very slowly rises to his feet. He feels the kind of tension that you could cut with a knife. The man doesn't have one yet, but he's working on it. He peers around the side of the shack to discover the deer. She's larger than life. The doe tilts her head to turn and look at the man, who is now standing in full view. After a few seconds, she rears herself back before prancing off into the wilderness. Impressively, she is much quieter when it counts.

With an amazed expression and feeling relieved, Joe returns to the back of the building and continues to bend the metal. After another couple minutes of creasing the four inches wide by twelve inches long triangle section, it separates from the rusty sheet. He touches the bottom of his index finger to the longest end of the triangular piece. It is sharp. He then rolls up the fragment, keeping the outermost point especially tight and feels it again cautiously with the fleshy part of his finger. He then wraps a length of vine around the bottom end. Joe has made a somewhat cone shaped shank. Relatively safe to grasp, it has its sharp point, is blunt at its handle end, and is rounded and narrow along its body. It is a decent weapon, given his current status. He slices at the air.

Inside the shack, he snatches the broom and returns outside. He lays the bristle end on the ground in front of himself, while cradling the handle end in his hands, he then puts his foot on the spot just above the broom end and pushes down hard. He slowly pulls up and toward himself on the handle. Joe trembles as he bends the wood with all his might. The broomstick breaks in half with a loud regrettable pop. He studies the broken end and is happy to find a sharp, narrow point on top, opposite the round end.

Inside, Joe places his makeshift, four-foot spear on the mattress and sets his cobbled together dagger beside it. He momentarily considers combining the two weapons but decides against the concept for the time being. He searches the shack one last time and once at the wardrobe, he picks up the books. He wipes the first one on his blue-and-green plaid shirt's sleeve. It is leather-bound and quite thick, with the title embossed into the front cover. '*Gone with the Wind.*' Joe puts it back and cleans off the second one. This one is black and heavily worn. "*Mein Kampf?*" he says to himself. He drops it to the floor and immediately regrets emitting another unnecessary noise. He stares at it a moment before retrieving it and commencing to tear out several pages and stuffing his every pocket.

Joe puts the wrecked book away, grabs his weapons and exits the shack.

He sets out southwest to where he heard the two gunshots.

After an hour or so, the clouds have completely taken over the sky, and from the overcast, it begins to drizzle ever so slightly. Joe looks up as he walks, catching some droplets on his face. It feels good. A little water on his skin is somehow soothing, but he can feel in the air that the worst of the downpour is yet to come.

As he carries on, the rainfall keeps a steady rushing sound inside the forest. It is calming to hear the sound of the rain. In a strange way, it makes him feel sheltered from danger, and it makes the woods seem smaller. Joe knows that the presence of rain comforting him is all in his head, but he is okay with that, for now.

Time continues to pass. He comes to a fork in the road where a gully splits the earth before him. He must decide whether to stay on the higher tier within the forest or venture lower, deeper into the woods. He examines the lay of the land more closely. The ground to his left, gradually flows down and the ground to his right steadily ascends up, but neither section appears too much more daunting than the other. Ultimately, he needs to continue southwest. So, Joe commits low, concluding that while higher ground is usually more ideal, the topside might take him too far west from where he heard the shots.

Constantly scanning as well as maintaining as much silence as possible and keeping good cover, Joe is confident that he has entered a zone in which something was fired at twice and that because both shots had been discharged so close together, there is a high probability that each bullet had successfully met with their common goal. Anxious to discover anything or anyone helpful, he is devoted in his search. He hopes to find people that can guide him to safe exit and not anyone looking to cause harm. He feels ready, nonetheless, to advance his situation, whatever the case may be. Joe creeps along the incline. He stops often to focus on his surroundings. The rain has subsided for the moment and left the forest cool and at peace.

Dusk begins to set in. Joe halts, squats down, and waits when he hears rustling amongst the bushes on ahead and down at the base of the cliff.

He can't identify any obvious movement. As he draws near, he begins to see it.

A juniper bush is shaking mildly, and before he can get closer, he hears a faint voice.

"Over here…" it calls. Joe waits. "Over here… It's okay, it's safe," says the meek voice.

Joe hurries over with his spear held out beside his body like a bayonet.

"No need for that… Not right now," says Charlie as Joe approaches.

He sticks his weapon into the earth and drops down to a crouch. Charlie is stretched out on his back underneath the juniper. He is mangled. He looks like he's been chewed up and spat out of a heavy machine and discarded.

"Oh man," says Joe. "Let's get you out from under there."

"No, no, first you must understand," urges Charlie as he turns through the pain to get a better look at Joe. "There is someone out there… And he is trying to kill us… He *is* killing us."

"I heard the shots," says Joe. "Let me get you out of there, and then we'll talk about that."

Joe cautiously pulls and guides Charlie out from the bush Charlie winces as he helps in the effort. Soon, he is free and sits there at the base of the infamous cliff. He has several injuries and is scraped and bruised. He needs stitches in numerous places, and his right arm, hand, leg, and foot are also badly wounded.

"I'm Charlie," he says.

"I'm Joe, nice to meet ya man," he returns the greeting and holds out his hand.

"I'm sorry Joe, but… I think my hand is fractured," says Charlie. He looks at his hand and then at his foot. "I'm pretty sure my ankle's not doing so well either. I had a similar stick," he adds, pointing out Joe's. "Musta lost it…when I fell."

Joe kneels down beside him

The two newly acquainted young men stare off into the distance longer than just to catch their breath. "You just happen by?" asks Charlie with a forced chuckle.

"Nah," Joe laughs. "Like I said, heard the shots."

Charlie smirks, he is oddly comforted to know that someone else he has met is alive and can attest to the clear and present danger.

"See the shooter?" asks Joe.

"Sure did… A little bit of him anyway. That's why I made my leap of faith. You wake up out here too? Joe? And were you alone or?"

"Yes, I did…and yes I was… What about you?"

Charlie shakes his head. "No, no, I did not. With me was a man—" he forces a smile.

"We should get further hidden," interrupts Joe. "I can see that this story is going to get worse, and we're losin' daylight fast. I don't wanna end up a part of this story for the next man to hear."

Charlie grimaces as he turns to Joe. "I'm not going anywhere and before you go, you need to listen to me."

"Charlie, you'll die here."

"You swear?" he asks, looking over to Joe.

"Look, I'm not leaving you here. As much as I want to hear about what you've been through and what's coming for us and I *do*, we need to get to safer ground first."

"I cannot go on, Joe. Here is where I will be. The pain is too much… I am so weak. I want to fall asleep and not wake up… You don't get it and besides, all I'll do now is slow you down."

"You can die wherever else you choose, whenever else you choose… But not here, not today…not on my watch," Joe asserts firmly.

Charlie shakes his head side to side. "You're not going away, are you?"

"No sir," says Joe as he rises and grabs Charlie's good hand and carefully brings him to his feet. Charlie winces, for a number of obvious reasons and others unnoticeable. He mutters under his breath. He had done a lot of whispering to himself since finding refuge under the bush. Even more so than normal.

"I suppose I'll have a great story to write if I make it outta here… A non-fiction too… Those are usually well-received."

"What's that?" says Joe.

Charlie thinks on whether or not to speak up or play it off. He decides to disclose his revelation. "I'm an aspiring writer…novels. If I don't make it, you'll have to write this story Joe, alright."

Joe wraps Charlie's arm around the back of his neck and takes his spear in hand. "Wow, that's admirable… I'd always had an interest in creative writing, tell you what…if I make it out and you don't, consider it done," Joe laughs. They make their way across the cliff to a thicker, better-covered area.

"And what do you do in real life?" asks Charlie.

"I'm a carpenter and I own a small contracting business."

"Oh, y'know, it's funny, I was always enthralled with wood shop."

They rest in a dense part of the forest, underneath a cluster of tall maple trees. Charlie is again on the ground and tells the story of Simon, the rickshaw, Neil, and the cherry tree. As Charlie tells his story, he digs out what cherries he can from his pockets and gives some to Joe who is nearby, on one knee with his spear stuck in the ground beside him.

He continues to speak of the massive marshland they discovered and their trip up the cliff where he endured his violent fall.

Charlie explains that when he was leaning to clean out the heel of his Nike, Neil noticed these certain types of trees.

"Neil made a good point," interjects Joe, Charlie pauses. "About identifying what we can and documenting our surroundings. I mean to help us understand where we are," he affirms.

"Yeah…that's another thing, about understanding…" Charlie snickers… "Where are you from Joe?"

"Upstate New York." Joe perks up. "You?" Joe is eager to hear Charlie's answer.

"Well, Upstate New York, I'm from Tampa Bay, Florida…the outskirts," he says sarcastically, as if that were to matter.

Joe closes his eyes tight and clenches them shut, as if painfully realizing all at once that they were even more trapped than he thought.

With dusk settling into the trees, Charlie continues on with the story, "Neil is pointing out this tree, that indicates that we are north and he points me in the direction to look, so I do and then I see him. A man dressed in a royal-blue cape, all trimmed in gold. He's got on this matching tunic and these fuckin' white pants. He's all decked out in clothes from I don't know what era. Like a...costume! My stomach sank because that big, blond, mustached maniac was aiming this golden rifle right at us. He appeared like a fuckin' phantom. I yelled out, but it was too late. He blasted Neil twice." Charlie's anger grows. "Right through his chest. He looked at me in so much disbelief before he dropped... Joe, nothing has ever made me feel so sorry for someone in all my life. I ran and jumped right off that cliff with all I had."

Both men go silent. Charlie chokes up and looks at Joe. "We're dead out here...*dead*...y'know?" he whispers. He shakes his head. Frustrated tears of confused rage roll down his face. They leave clean lines through the thin residue of dirt on his cheeks.

"Yeah, well... Like I said, not today, Charlie," confirms Joe with determination. He looks away, so as to not allow himself to get choked up too.

"Joe, I believe that a man dies many deaths throughout his life... the trials, tribulations, and tragedies we all have to endure from time to time... those are deaths, not just...disappointments, sadness, or broken hearts."

They sit in silence looking through the trees and up the cliff.

"That man killed me in my backyard," announces Charlie.

Moments pass before Joe speaks, breaking the silence. "Let's go Charlie," he says as the Sun is just about set.

With a roll of thunder surrounding them, the two men rise to their feet and slowly disappear eastward, into the ever-darkening forest.

# 12

# In the Mist

The sky is gray and gloomy. A slight rain follows the thunderstorm from the night before and descends lightly onto the woods.

A man is steadily plucking and devouring raspberries off of a small bush. Thunder rumbles again and a flash of lightning illuminates the area. Clive looks up as he eats. He is damp, and dirty, his fingers are red from the berry juice. He's been picking a while and been taking his time in getting every last bit of fruit. He finishes and looks up again. The rain is tapering off to a mist. It's as if it is coming from the trees themselves as it relentlessly swirls within the new day's warming atmosphere. He examines the forest with his eyes for a direction that might present the most promise.

Clive shakes his head fast to dispel some water from his hair and proceeds northwest through nature's labyrinth.

He walks a while, and as he does, he tries to piece together the last days leading up to his abduction. He is groggy and sore. The fright he had experienced the night before exchanged with ambition for the day ahead. He is anxious to get out of the woods, but knows, he must not let the mystery of his reality lead him to panic. Clive walks well. Stopping every so often to search his surroundings for easier passage within the thicket or safe shelter from the strange mist. He pushes on all day, relatively confident that he'll find civilization soon. Though otherwise suppressed, potential bouts of negative rumination aggravatingly surface now and then, they are mostly left unexamined and kept in the back of his mind and ignored like a scab that mustn't be scratched. He's been studying the greenery since dawn broke and feels that he could be somewhere near his home and is comforted by the possibility.

*They picked me up and dumped me in the woods... But why?* He thinks to himself. *After all, I did have a couple of hundred bucks on me. It was an elaborate mugging!* He says aloud sarcastically. His heart sinks because he is certain that two hundred dollars, an old cellphone, and a sporty wristwatch wouldn't be enough reason for a group of people to assault, mug, perhaps drug, and kidnap someone.

Increasingly more bewildered, he glances at his bare wrist where his watch should be and is all the more frustrated. He stops and looks around. Clive is growing paranoid as the sky stirs above. Carrying forward and moving quicker now, he ventures on. He climbs over rocks, through bushes, up hills and down. The man is soaked and scraped as he walks to a clearing through a patch of daisies.

Through the haze of the rain, he identifies a shack. Despite some nervousness, he is excited to see a second building and jogs toward it. Anything other than trees and brush is a sight for sore eyes. He gets closer and slows back down to a walk. He can't believe his eyes, as he analyzes the shack. After all that hiking, through so much of the day and he has simply arrived back around to the very building he had woken up in. Clive picks up his pace again and enters it fast, as if it might actually be a different shack if he crosses its threshold quickly. He shakes his head over and over in disbelief. His eyes are wide with shock. Clive's shelter has only a single mattress that lays in the corner soiled and drab. Dejected, he sits on an overturned end table by the door and studies the bedding. "It can't be," he whispers in disbelief.

Clive peers beyond the doorway and southeast to where he came from, in awe at the fact that he had somehow actually gotten himself turned around and made it all the way back by pure mistake. He is ashamed and disgusted with himself. He lowers his head. The floor at his feet is severely rotten, exposing the earth beneath. He stares through a large void between the decrepit floorboards at the ground below, trying to regain some hope.

The young man decides that tomorrow he will take his chances by travelling northwest and pay strict attention as he does, perhaps even leave some sort of markers if he gets mixed up again.

Clive stands outside a moment. He climbs the stout shack, carefully checking the roof's structure before pulling himself on top. He marvels at having gotten lost within being lost. He pushes the deep, excruciating thought from his mind and looks all around very slowly as the rain's mist continues to envelope him. It is so dense now, as if he were set there in a boat on a lake, surrounded by large waterfalls. He shields his eyes and stares northwest, mentally preparing himself for the next morning's trek. Back in the building, Clive is confronted by the challenge of the rainfall's mist pouring in through the gaping doorway. He doesn't particularly like the idea of getting soaked all night, on top of his already very difficult set of circumstances. So he proceeds to flip over the mattress, which releases from the floor with a tear; they had both been fused together by decades of neglect. He drags it over to the doorway and leans it on its side lengthways on a slant, as to block some of the encroaching water. He then slides the end table to the mattresses center, so it doesn't blow over. Clive lays down on his back beside his cobbled together partition wall.

As evening sets in, the mist wafts in from his left, through the space above the mattress and above him and the end-table, but it passes by and dissipates into the air inside the shack. Clive is comforted that he is at least somewhat sheltered from the elements.

It is darker now but not completely. He begins to dwell on his harsh reality as he looks up at the shoddy ceiling of his den. He grows more and more sickened as time passes, until he finally resists thinking about his situation negatively. His confusion and frustration is replaced with daydreams of people and places beyond the forest. He fantasizes about meeting people that can help him within the woods, and even what the roads and towns may look like beyond the green boundaries when he discovers them. He considers the prospect of civilization being incredibly close, should he simply just pick the right direction.

After a while of deep thought, Clive scans the floor. He recalls that he never really searched the dresser beyond tripping over it when he woke in a panic and then sliding it to the mattress for support just recently. Both times however, it did feel empty. He reaches over across himself and opens the bottom drawer with his right hand and fishes around inside, there is nothing.

He turns and props himself up on his left elbow for better leverage and checks the top drawer. He finds a large piece of old newspaper lining the bottom. It is yellowed and brittle. Clive lays back down and scans the portion. There is just enough light left to read it. He searches for locations or dates. There are none. With the last remnants of daylight slipping away, he holds the paper closely above his face, but his focus drifts away from the page. He ponders about how long he'd been there in the woods and considers the notion that he might have been there much longer than a day or two, that maybe the same confusing forest that had miraculously brought him after a full, days walk back to where he started could be the same confusing forest that could twist time itself. After all, time is but a man-made construct. Perhaps it's not June...*perhaps*...it's not even 2012... He aggressively shakes the thought and adjusts his eyes back to the newspaper. There are two partially legible articles.

One column, beginning at the top-left corner with a missing heading, reads 'outstanding decrease of mosquitoes within the area.' *Wherever this is,* he thinks. It has poorly structured excerpts from locals, like; 'Clifford from Jack's Hardware' said it's: 'Like nothing he can recall,' and 'Betty from Bluebonnet Bakery' said: 'Can't complain, though!' He grimaces at the simplicity of the article but imagines Clifford and Betty and feels a little comfort in the idea that maybe he's in a place that is not all bad, a simple place. The comfort is short-lived. Not too simple, he hopes to himself. *Not 'Deliverance' simple...more 'Little House on the Prairie' simple*. It doesn't alleviate his frustration that neither Jack's hardware nor Bluebonnet bakery are recognizable establishments... The place the forest has taken his mind to is infecting his clarity. While over-thinking might help him behind a team bench, he tells himself to be less a coach under these circumstances and more a player. For *that* role one must be more instinctual than analytical. He decides he needs to apply that strategy *here*, in the woods.

The second column, on the bottom-right with no ending, is about conservation areas.

'What to expect when in the wild. What to pack and when to rest during extended visits and other pleasantries.' Clive thinks it to be terribly ironic. It's just about too dark to read when a big gust of wind blows into his shack, bringing plenty of rain with it, and taking his paper as it enters the doorway. Clive is left with an insignificant fragment in his hand. He slowly sets it down beside himself. The rain is becoming heavier and forces Clive to squeeze in and lay on his side as close to the mattress as possible, almost hugging the end table. He covers his ears and remains still.

He thinks about Betty and her bakery and what goods she would have. He hopes she's still there. Clive travels space and time and imagines an exceptionally kind and outgoing woman, as they talk at her glass counter. It is filled with cakes, pies, and pastries. Clifford enters and joins them there. The bakery then turns into the hardware store, transforming all around the three individuals. The counter's shelving now filled with tool-belts, saw-blades, and drill bits. He begins talking about how the lack of mosquitoes is "Like nothing he can recall," to which Betty replies: "Can't complain though!"

Before long, his imaginations turn from the locals to his grandmother and the times they'd shared together in the past and even the fresh-baked lasagna she'd make in her kitchen for the extended family, when he was a boy.

Within his head, Clive finally finds himself at a place where he feels safe and at ease. He holds onto the emotion and stays seated with her at her kitchen table and before long, he is fast asleep.

The next morning brings about relatively clear skies. The rainfall has moved on and warmer breezes are flowing through the woods. Clive removes his barricade and drinks awhile from a deep puddle near the shack that had formed in the night.

He sets out northwest with a heavy heart. He feels decent enough, though and slept well, considering his ordeal. He is optimistic about the new day and the opportunities it could bring.

Clive walks with determination as the Sun's appearance becomes more and more prominent. His distorted clothes are almost dry. A minor discomfort, one that he has nonetheless been anticipating putting behind him with great relish. His black 'Super Star Sports' polo shirt is especially battered. There is a large rip under the red 'SSS' logo. He walks on with his arm across his chest and his hand gripping the bottom of the tear. Later, up about thirty yards, Clive sees another shack. Certain this time that it is not the one he was dumped in—the one to which he came back to the day before when he so unfortunately made an unexpected backtrack.

He is overcome with excitement and the potential that his new discovery might prove helpful in some way. When Clive arrives at the building, he begins to explore it. He looks at the two single beds pushed together. Other than the sheet-less, pillow-less, and rather putrid mattresses, this particular shack houses little else and nothing significant sets it apart from his. He wonders about the beds…why they're there, in a similar building to the one he woke up in…and why two? He is awkwardly both elated and horrified about the existence of another building and the possibility of others being present in the woods. Clive exits the shack. He feels an elevated sense of responsibility and focuses only on positive thoughts. As he passes by the structure, he does not notice the bloodstained, faded-yellow Pennzoil hat suspended within the tall grass behind it. After a few seconds, he disappears, further northwest bound, down a hill and deeper into the forest.

# 13
# Seeking Allies

Another night dragged on with blustering wind and intermittent rainfall, yet again. Charlie and Joe carefully traversed the forest as best they could and slept under a giant weeping willow with ample shelter. The morning sunshine's full effects saturate parts of the great tree and from it, a subtle, pale green ambiance is cast underneath. They have decided to stay put and calculate their next move. The cover and comfort the willow provides is difficult for the pair to simply leave behind, so they take advantage and bask within the green haze.

"There have got to be others," says Charlie.

"We need to find them," proclaims Joe.

"I can keep walking Joe, but barely," announces Charlie as he points to his ankle. It had swelled considerably during the night.

Joe thinks for a moment. "If there's a killer out there and you are growing increasingly immobile… I think I may have a temporary solution."

"Alright, what is it?"

"Okay… So, if we were put here in these buildings, then who's to say that we will be searched for *inside* of them? It's plausible that one could hide in plain sight for a while."

"*Or*," adds Charlie… "One could assume the role of the sitting duck…lucky for me, either outcome sounds fine."

"So, let's hope we find a shed, where I can hole up huh."

"Not quite," says Joe. "If we choose to do this, we go back to mine, I'm certain it isn't too far off and I was there enough to know it wasn't being watched. While you rest there and heal, I'll search for food, any other people that might be here, as well as a way out of these woods."

"I suppose it's worth a try," agrees Charlie. "Let's go for it."

"I need to know you're sure though, I'm just thinking of the best way to handle our current situation."

"I am sure Joe, at this point, it's all a gamble anyway, and I gotta get off my feet for a while before I can't move at all. You just make sure you come back."

"I will."

The two men, however reluctantly, leave the solace of the weeping willow and do well reaching Joe's shack. Charlie lays out on the bed.

"If I get it, at least it will be in *here* and not in the bush." He musters a smile.

"I *will* come back," affirms Joe. He lays his broomstick spear beside Charlie. "Sit tight," he says and takes his exit. He walks back inside, instantaneously opens the wardrobe, and tosses Charlie '*Gone with the Wind.*'

Surprised after he reads the title, he looks at Joe and raises his eyebrows.

Joe shrugs, smiles slightly and disappears through the doorway again.

With ambitious determination, he heads due east. He figures that since south wasn't good, because of the vast marshlands, and west had proved to have been bad luck, he might as well set out east. He travels an hour or so, always listening, watching, and minding the details that will lead him back to Charlie. Joe surveys a shallow pond as it comes into full view. He begins to wonder the extent of the marshland Charlie and Neil had discovered. He wonders just how far and wide it *is* and whether or not it may be conquerable. He wants to trust their judgment, but he doesn't know Charlie well and didn't even meet Neil at all. *There's gotta be a safe passage somewhere in there, be it east, or west, or ever deeper south*, he thinks.

Joe kneels down, reaches into the pond, and takes a handful of water to his lips. It's cool and fresh with rainwater.

The morning air is clearer than the days before, as the early summer sunshine peeks in and out of a collection of cumulus clouds. Joe finishes drinking to find, in front of him about fifteen yards away, on the other side of the pond, another doe. He blinks his eyes in quick succession, as if she may vanish into thin air, but she does not.

Upon inspection, he notices familiar markings on the deer and wonders if this visitor is the same one he saw before near his shed. He is overcome with a feeling of contentment as they watch each other. The doe steps carefully, walking closer to the edge of the water, never taking it's eye of Joe, and takes a drink. Joe looking back, slowly does the same. Suddenly the animal's ears and tail point upward and as quickly as she appeared, she bounds off again and is gone.

Joe waits to find out if what prompted his friend to flee is a threat to him too. Soon, when he is comfortable, he commences his solo venture, particularly observing landmarks and sticking pretty closely to a straight line, even when curving around a tree or hole or when he climbs over a rock or boulder. He is savvy in the bush and knows that he needs to operate efficiently, if he is to thrive and succeed in the forest. Before long, Joe stumbles upon an aged tree house, just to the south of his chosen route, way up high in an oak tree. It looks about twenty or thirty years old and in much better shape than the infamous shacks. It is obvious that *this* shelter was built with quality materials and was a labor of love, opposite of the thrown together, cheap stylings of the shack where Charlie lays. There are two feet long, two-by-six pieces of lumber, nailed horizontally, every few feet along the tree. They start at the tree trunk and continue on, leading all the way up to the tree house. Joe carefully climbs up the ladder to investigate. He's eager to get a look at the lay of land from on high and considers the possibility of this being an even better resting place for his new friend Charlie until they can reach proper safety.

Joe studies the landscape westward from the top of the ladder before climbing over into the small open window, serving as the doorway on the west side of the structure from the top of the ladder. He carefully puts his left leg in first while using his right one for leverage on the last two-by-six-step. Inside, Joe is gut-wrenched by what he sees. The tree house is a hollow cube no bigger than thirty square feet and barely tall enough for even a child to stand in. It has a single wooden stool bolted to the floorboards in the center and there is one four-inch hole cut perfectly into the middle of each wall minus the one with the window. In front of Joe on the opposite wall from the entrance, there are block letters in faded white paint:

**'YOU'RE NOT IN KANSAS ANYMORE.'**

Joe's head spins, crouching down in a crow's nest…quite likely, the very location where a twisted pursuer has been set and perched… waiting on the stool with their firearm clutched in their hands, watching through the holes, indulging in the prospect of ambushing and dispatching of an innocent victim in cold-blood. Sharing in a space with quite possibly whomever had terrorized Joe's predecessors sends shivers down his spine. He trembles at first when his stomach sinks, but the feeling is quickly replaced with adrenaline-infused rage. He bends down further to look out through the hole to his immediate right on the south side first, then moves along to the left to the east, and finally the north. Joe is about fifty feet from ground level, not nearly high enough to study up beyond the tree line, or even into a substantial distance, but high enough to get some good looks down at the landscape spread out before him in all immediate directions.

There wasn't much to see through the first two holes, but the third hole serves as the best one. His jaw drops while he's looking out the north side and discovers the steel roof of another shack about one-hundred yards ahead in the distance. The shiny silver metal pops within its vast, green surroundings. He looks out the window, scans the area west again for a moment, and climbs down. Joe aggressively navigates the woods, excited to reach the newest building.

He does his best to keep his composure, as he can no longer see it from ground level and must anxiously follow his nose in the green maze.

After about an hour, Joe finds the shack. It is a lot like the others from the outside, with small, insignificant differences inside. Nothing telling is there but a single bed.

Joe is confident that someone else like him and Charlie is in the forest. Maybe more than one, running and hiding and running some more. Perhaps looking for others, just as he is.

He is certain it's not Charlie and Simon's shack, because Charlie had mentioned there being two beds and a nearby creek. He understands that it could have been Neil's, but holds out hope that it's someone else's. Joe sits inside, on the bed and figures it could be a longshot but decides to wait anyway, at least a couple of hours. If there is anyone, they might not be straying too far from their building yet. He thinks of Charlie as he waits and hopes he's okay, he had not heard any shots and that's incredibly comforting. Joe hopes he will not be waiting in vain. He lays down on the bed and stares up at the ceiling and through a gap in the roof. He looks at the trees above as they gently sway.

Joe is always observing the forest.

Time passes. He continues to think of Charlie and home until he slowly starts to fall asleep. He snaps out of it and sits himself up on the mattress and leans his back against the wall. At least if something *does* present itself, he'll be facing it. He takes out his steel shank from under his belt and rests his eyes. He fights the urge to fall to slumber again and concentrates on the sounds around him.

Soon after, something indeed does come slowly creeping into the shack...

Joe's eyes focus on the doorway as he squeezes the handle of his weapon... A man appears, puts his hands up, and holds his palms facing Joe.

"I'm Clive," Joe stands up and dusts off his shoulders and the seat of his pants with his free hand. He looks Clive up and down. "Are you a friend?" he asks, as he points the dagger toward the tear in Clive's shirt.

"I am," he replies.

Joe holsters his weapon under his belt and tells his new companion to drop his hands.

"Where are you from, Clive?"

"Portland, Oregon."

"I'm from Upstate New York. How long you been here in the wilderness?"

"Three days… I think."

"You see anyone else? Or hear any gunshots?"

"No, I've been searching these woods, trying to get out. It's impossible. It's a goddamn maze."

"There are others… It's a possibility that we're being hunted. You need to come with me and meet Charlie. We all need to band together if we wanna get out of this alive," says Joe firmly.

"You and this Charlie? Were you guys taken and left here too?"

"Yes, but we need to move. Charlie will fill you in once we get there. We are not alone, and we're running out of time. We're starving, and thirsty and someone with a rifle…maybe even a sniper rifle, is out here… Come on, if we move quietly and carefully, we should be there in a few hours."

"Where?" asks Clive.

"To the shed *I* woke up in. That's where Charlie is."

The men waste not another second and start out.

# 14

# Back South

Charlie lay inside the shack. The man is white. He wakes from his deep sleep, slowly, to find Joe and their newest member standing over him.

"*Whoa,*" whispers Clive as he looks upon the battered individual before him. "Charlie, I'm Clive," he says as he briefly puts his hand on Charlie's shoulder.

"Wow... Another one, huh?" grunts Charlie. "That's good... That's good... I guess...well...not for *you*," he says as he struggles to sit up. Clive fidgets and looks to Joe with an expression of immediate concern. Charlie catches his questionable choice of words. "I mean, it is good depending upon one's perspective." He looks down at his foot, his ankle is getting worse as time passes. It is clear, that it needs medical attention.

"You're a writer?" asks Joe both sarcastically and rhetorically. "What he means Clive is that it's good we've found one another, so we can work together to get out and that it's not so good that you're here all together." Joe looks back to Charlie and shakes his head side to side. "Does that about cover it?"

"It does," replies Charlie. "Thank you for the amendments." He continues...

"Nice to make your acquaintance."

"Did you tell him what's going on?" Charlie asks as he looks at Joe.

"He knows there is someone out there. I wanted you to tell him the rest," discloses Joe.

Charlie winces and pulls himself further up, to lean his upper-back and head on the wall behind him. For a split-second he imagines Simon in Clive's place, standing over him with rock in hand. Joe notices the brief fleck of anguish in Charlie's eyes.

"I know we're all in this together, but I thought he should hear it from you."

"Yes… Yes, I understand," agrees Charlie, forcing a somber smile. "They are my stories to tell."

Clive leans on the wardrobe attentively and the injured Charlie begins. He methodically divulges an uncut version of the events that lead him up to the minute of their meeting.

Clive feels sick after being updated about everything that has transpired.

He understands that they are in grave danger, having heard all about the murders and he realizes how suddenly death could actually come to any of them, at any moment. The urgency to leave the woods is extremely prominent for him now.

"So, what do we do boys?" Clive asks as he searches their eyes for answers.

"All we can do is continue to tread carefully and hope for the best. Hope to find freedom beyond, as soon as possible, and we need to keep looking for more men as we go," explains Joe.

"I've been way south," grunts Charlie as he slouches. "And even west too."

"Yes, but just how far?" asks Joe without waiting for an answer. "We need to pick one direction and stick with it. We're running out of time here."

"I've been east awhile," adds Clive. "What about north?" he suggests.

"The two times we were shot at, the killer had approached us from the north," says Charlie.

"But who's to say where he'll be next time he attacks us?" says Clive.

"It's true," agrees Joe. "Could be a worthwhile endeavor."

"Yeah, it could be worth a shot…or two, or three shots even. One for each of us," says Charlie.

"Well, we gotta pick one direction and go with it. No matter what, searching all directions in spurts isn't cutting it."

"I agree Joe, I agree it's worth a try, that we should walk a straight line right outta here, I do. But I can't do that, not yet…so just go on ahead and don't look back." Clive looks on and holds his tongue. He's too new to say anything about the dilemma between Joe and Charlie.

"How much time do you need?" asks Joe.

"For what?" asks Charlie.

"To heal enough to where you can put sufficient pressure on that foot?"

Charlie chuckles, "Four to six weeks."

"Really, Charlie, I'm serious here," demands Joe.

"So am I." A moment passes. "Gimme tonight," answers Charlie. He looks at both men standing over him. "Gimme tonight," he repeats.

Joe and Clive set out south as Charlie lays resting.

"You told Charlie we were going north awhile, to scout things."

"I know, Clive, but the man's got his share to worry about. This is not the time to second-guess his judgment too much, and I wanna get a look at the wetlands for myself. I *need* to see if there's any promise to them at all. If we can possibly get through them or around them. It might lead us somewhere, it must... I know it sounds like a lot, but no mad man is gonna follow us through miles of marshland, let alone care to look for us in there." A moment passes while the pair walks in silence.

Clive pipes up. "But what if it doesn't lead anywhere...for a hundred miles?"

"I need to see it," replies Joe. "I need to lay eyes on it. Our lives depend on it. I need to see for myself, if there's a chance out there."

They walk in silence a moment more.

"Okay Joe, I'm with you," affirms Clive.

The men head through the forest efficiently, working together well and paying attention to each other's body language when remotely separated and they only talk when absolutely necessary.

They reach a clearing and stay low to the ground within the wide-open space and cross the desolate area without hesitation. Their focus is always sharp.

Clive reaches the thicket on the other side first and picks up a tarnished, two hundred and fifty milliliter clear glass bottle from the grass at the divide. Joe arrives shortly after. They stop within the trees.

Clive holds the bottle up, showing off his find.

Joe nods in approval.

As they get going into the woods and deeper south, there are prominent sounds of movement in the trees above.

"Squirrels or the like," says Joe as he uses his dagger to point directly upward. Clive nods in agreement as they creep on through the dense shrubbery below.

Slowly but surely, after about an hour of traversing the thick, rolling landscape, it flattens out and leads the men to the southernmost reach of the woods. They remain still as they peer out from the forest's low-laying perimeter into vast, seemingly un-ending marshlands. They stretch out as far as the eye can see. It is an unforgiving green abyss, brimming with dark waterways, massive, muddy swamps and countless brown tipped cattails, carrying on south as well as east and west. The collective drone of varying species blankets the wetlands.

"Charlie was right," says Clive as they look beyond.

"Yeah," agrees Joe. "What the hell are we gonna do?" he asks, to no response.

"It would be suicide if we ventured out there… Wouldn't it?" he adds.

"Yeah, it would be," answers Clive, finally. There is an obvious hint of despondence in his tone.

"Let's head back," says Joe. He is extremely disappointed.

"Wait," says Clive as he pulls the bottle from his back pocket. He kneels down, fills it with water, shakes it, and pours it out and fills it again. It is slightly murky.

"Bottoms up," he says upon rising and tipping it back.

He lobs the bottle to his friend. Joe bends down and fills it.

He examines the antique coke bottle and its contents, guzzles the cool water all the way down, and returns the toss, back to Clive, who then fills it back up to about three-quarters. He grabs a large leaf from a nearby bush, stuffs it into the nozzle, and steadily puts the bottle back in his pocket. They return to the woods and head north.

On their way back to Charlie, they quietly exchange stories of their lives left behind. Joe speaks of his building business and his family. His brothers and sisters, his mother and father, nieces and nephews. He even mentions his dog and shudders at the thought of him sleeping at the front door tirelessly waiting for his master to come home.

Clive talks about his college years, sports obsession, coaching record, old friends, and past loves. As they converse about home, experiences, and simple blessings, they never speak in past tense. Joe especially expresses plans for when he gets back home regarding his intentions for a personal relationship that he longingly intends to repair.

Later, the afternoon sun is settling down as the two press on in silence. When the shelter comes into view, Joe stops and gently puts his arm out to halt Clive's stride.

"Don't tell Charlie we checked back south," he urges. "Tell him we poked around north and that it was safe… I don't want to disappoint him, he's had enough of those."

"Sure," says Clive, "I understand Joe."

They arrive inside the shack and Charlie is fast asleep. He wakens to find Joe and Clive sitting on the floor. Clive looks at Charlie as Joe keeps steady watch through the doorway.

Clive smiles. "Hey buddy!" he says. "Gotcha something." He removes the leaf cork and passes over the murky bottle of water. Charlie grabs it and proceeds to drinking most of it.

"Take her in," says Clive as he pats his stomach. "I'm good, she's all yours."

"Wow," says Charlie, once finished. "You find a vending machine out there?" he asks.

They laugh.

"No luck to speak of, huh?" adds Charlie.

"Nope," replies Joe. "But you know what they say, no news is good news."

Charlie sets the bottle on the floor beside the bed and rolls back toward the wall. Dusk has almost fully set in, and the night's creatures are gradually beginning to stir.

Joe doesn't bat an eye, as he continues to look beyond and into the dark woods.

"I got first watch," he says, staring deeply into the oblivion.

# 15
# Unification

Nighttime had come to pass quite peacefully. The men had executed their spontaneous 'night watch' strategy efficiently, alternating back and forth, and even Charlie took a substantial shift.

Dawn breaks with Joe on watch. Shortly after Charlie wakes, Clive does too. The men talk about their hunger. It is becoming excruciating. Joe and Clive consider the possibilities of hunting for some food and their appetite quickly escalates to fantasies of cooked meat. Once they can finally pull themselves together, they narrow down which route to travel, with north, northwest, and northeast being their options to mull over. Northwest wins out as their chosen direction. They figure if need be, they can adjust their path as they go if they must, but they know for sure that south is most definitely out of the equation.

The men are about to begin when Joe spots a couple of people approaching from afar. They remain in the shack and quickly take cover. The two strangers disappear in and out of view as they advance the woods steadily from the southeast. To stay hidden, Charlie sits by the bed. Clive leans in a corner, and Joe takes the place beside the doorframe. He maintains a good vantage point from which to observe the encroaching figures.

They hold their breath. Joe takes out his dagger and Charlie passes the spear to Clive. The two men clutch their weapons tight. The strangers are close now and clearly coming toward the shack.

"One big guy and one little guy," whispers Joe. "No guns visible, no weapons," he says as the travelers gain even more ground. "I think they're our guys," he says. "Yeah... They're not dressed for a walk in the wilderness," says Joe.

Roebuck and Willy appear to be in good spirits.

Joe steps out and puts his hand up casually. The shorter man waves back as they jog to the shelter. Willy looks especially positive.

Clive looks at Charlie with a smile. Charlie shakes his head side to side and exhales the breath he had been holding.

"Howdy! There are more of us, huh? Hot dang, I knew it!" cheers Willy.

"Hey boys," drawls Roebuck rather calmly.

"Jesus, how many of us are out here?" says Joe excitably.

"I'm Joe, this is Clive, and that there is Charlie," he says as he points to the bed. The two groups of newly acquainting men are stood on either side of the doorway.

"Willy, y'all! Good to meetchyas!"

"Roebuck," says the large man, nodding to the others.

"Yeah, strange name, huh? Reminds me of a boat!" exclaims Willy.

"You mean an oar?" asks Roebuck with a playful grin, in an effort to slip up his companion.

"Nah man, I keep tellin' ya, a boat! Don't ya get it yet?"

Joe and Clive look at each other, then at Roe. He lifts his eyebrows and then looks at Willy, almost proudly.

Willy elaborates, "I've been callin' him Rowboat," he snorts.

"Because my name sounds like rowboat, very clever," says Roe.

"Well that, and you're as big as a boat," replies Willy.

"Boats can be small ya know."

"No, they can't."

"Sure, they can, friend. There are coracles, kayaks, peddle boats, jet skis…"

"Alight, alright," interrupts Willy.

Roe continues, "…lil' airboats, banana boats…dinghies."

Clive motions to Willy's large partially scabbed wound, which draws a line down his forehead from his hairline. "That where they got ya?" he asks.

"Sure did, sons a' bitches," returns Willy without missing a beat. "Hey, that reminds me," he adds, "I'm from Santa Fe, New Mexico, and this big bear roams the country-side of Salt Lake City, Utah! Can you believe that shit! How 'bout you boys?" asks Willy. The men answer one by one, as if especially tired of that *particular* conundrum.

"New York," says Joe.

"Oregon," says Clive.

"Florida," adds Charlie.

"Goddamn! What in the fuck is up with that?" says Willy, exuberantly.

"How long you two been out here?" asks Joe.

"Prit' near four days or so, eh Rowboat?" says Willy.

"Sounds about right… Three, four days," agrees Roe. "Maybe five," he adds. "It's all becoming a blur."

"Were you guys together?" asks Charlie.

"Sure were. I woke up and this big brute was laid down beside me in his baby-blue pajamas. I didn't know what to think!" says Willy.

"They took me in the middle of the night," announces Roe, as he looks down at his simple, thin, pale blue pants and long sleeve shirt. He clears out some small, broken twigs and other debris from the front pocket, then briefly examines and scratches a small bug bite on the underside of his wrist. "Speaking of night time, it's a darn good thing the mosquitos haven't been too awful. I expected to be overrun after dark." The men inside the shack notice Roebuck's wrapped feet and Joe pipes up. "You obviously didn't have shoes on."

"Nope, but thanks to ol' Willy here for the donation of his under shirt. Sure helped the cause." The large man has torn a white cotton t-shirt in half and wrapped and tied the material tightly around each of his bare feet with extra emphasis placed on his soles. Each make-shift shoe is heavily soiled and tattered, but so far, he walks well.

The men are empathetic to the man's specific handicap and the collective silence endorses their feelings further. Finally, Charlie breaks the tension and replaces it with a newer more intense concern.

"You hear any gunshots?"

"Nuh-uh," answers Willy. "Why? Have you fellas?"

Joe looks to Charlie. Charlie forces a smile from where he sits and begins, "I woke up with someone too…" he proceeds to elaborate on everything they don't know and enlighten them about their harsh reality.

When he finishes, all five men are quiet again.

"FUCKERS!" yells Willy passionately, causing Charlie to jolt.

"I thought we were abducted by sickos, but this? We're in deep lads," says Roe in his composed way of speaking.

"What have you guys been doing all this time?" asks Joe.

"Walking the land. Yeah, we knew we were in danger big time, but we didn't know what the hell was going on for sure, so we been tryna' just get the hell to a road or a town; the forest seems endless. Pretty crazy, but after a few days of not seein' a soul, we've been gettin' a bit big for our britches, too comfortable maybe.

"We've been wandering northwest. We haven't found a whole lot of potential anywhere we go," admits Roebuck.

"Tell me about it," concurs Joe.

Willy chimes back in. "I had climbed a few tall trees to see what I could see but, couldn't get high enough to see anything worth a damn. Just more forest."

"Hey, what's in the bag?" asks Clive, pointing to a small burlap sack slung over Willy's shoulder and around his back.

"Ohhh boys!" he exclaims. "A dead rabbit," he says. His tone of voice and facial expression is immediately serious.

Clive looks shocked.

"Why," he asks, somewhat afraid for what he might hear. "Don't tell me you have been…eating it."

"Sure!" replies Willy, "you want some?" He livens back up. Clive looks at Joe, then at Charlie. "It ain't just rabbit, I got a whole load a' cherries in here too! Me and Rowboat happened by a cherry tree and picked it clean! Well…what of it we could reach. Filled this here bag!"

"It's dead rabbit…and cherries?" says Charlie.

"Yepper!"

"I don't know," says Clive.

"You kill it, the rabbit?" inquires Joe.

"Nope, found it!" Willy beams with pride.

Joe looks at Rowboat. "You eatin' any?"

"I'm starving, and I'm weak. But no, I have not," he answers.

"It's fresh," claims Willy. "It ain't spoiled, or smellin' or nothin'!"

The conversation changes tone as all the men sit around the shack and relax. They talk for a while, each with their own varying dialect and differing accent. The group reset what little plans and expectations they have and after considering their collective experiences within the forest, they opt to venture straight north. It is the only direction no one has tried yet, beyond their location and they all agree not to divert from the plan unless absolutely necessary.

"I have got to go and test this foot for a minute or two. Warm it up," announces Charlie. Roebuck suggests they wrap it with a shirt before they head out, invoking his intimate connection to the idea.

Joe highlights with the rest of the men what they surely already know…that everybody needs to stay sharp and relatively quiet, to always keep an ear to the ground and their head on a swivel. Even if he is stating the obvious, he feels it certainly can't hurt to do so and hearing it should only raise the group's collective morale.

He watches as Charlie walks around, shaking his foot as if he'd just been bean balled in the ankle by a major league pitchers wild throw. The player, testing his foot outside the batter's box while the other men wait in the field for the game to resume.

"This guy we're dealing with seems to be a crack shot. Y'know what I'm sayin?"

"No worries," says Roebuck. "We gotta work together. All for one."

"Yeah, we hear ya man," says Willy.

Joe averts his eyes behind Charlie, across a clearing and into the distant woods. Out of the tree line, southeast of the shack, a man appears like a specter. He's got on black boots, white pants, and a red wool waistcoat with gold trim along the front. A high collar and long sleeve cuffs protrude from within his coat. He wears a big, black hat with yellow trim, and a coin dangles from a small rope string on the hat's front-left side. He has a golden sword attached at his hip. It is a uniform from the Napoleonic era. He is a tall, thin, elderly man and has a wrinkled, tanned face with a rather large, sun bleached-blond handlebar mustache that is twisted up on each side. It is impressively obvious that he is fit for his age as he marches a few feet from the trees and points a large rifle in Charlie's direction. Joe's eyes dilate as he looks upon their living nightmare.

"CHARLIE!" he shouts at the top of his lungs.

The man pulls the trigger. Smoke comes out of the barrel and the gun bellows loudly through the forest as it blasts. The bullet catches Charlie in his abdomen and exits through his lower back. He twists around as he falls flat on his front side. He faces the men as they scatter north as fast as they can. They all take off, but Joe stays behind. "Charlie!" he calls again.

Charlie looks right into Joe's eyes. "Go!" he shouts.

The shooter, now speed walking toward Charlie, reloads and fires up into the air as if to back Joe away and quickly reloads again.

Still staring at one another with conviction in their eyes, Charlie nods to Joe.

Joe is frozen for a second and then turns and runs to join the rest of the men. He catches up with Roe and stops him briefly. Clive and Willy are up ahead a fair distance and do not break their running stride as they flee. "Go in a straight line from here, three hundred yards, try to get the others' attention and wait for me. I'll be there soon."

"What of it?" asks Roe.

"I gotta watch this bastard, see where he goes from here, if I can."

"Joe?" says Roebuck with concern in his voice.

"It's okay, I'll be okay. Now, go, don't let them lose us… I'll be there!"

Roe turns and continues running down the invisible path toward the rest of the men.

Joe sneaks up alongside the shack. He squats down to witness the lanky man towering over his friend and as he kicks his latest victim in the ribs with all of his might, he is stone-faced. Charlie gasps as he rolls over. The man steps over him with a boot on either side of his hips. He holds up his rifle and examines the end of its barrel. It smolders subtly. He then peers out into the forest in front of him. He feels as if the whole world belongs to him. He breathes the entire forest in deep, while closing his eyes and opens them as he slowly exhales it. He turns his attention back to Charlie and looks him up and down. He studies his catch for a moment and then mercilessly guides the end of his rifle down to Charlie's forehead. He presses the barrel of his gun against it firmly. Charlie glares up into the killer's eyes, in anger. "Do it."

Joe turns away as the shot rings out. He drops his head and closes his eyes. Sorrow for his innocent friend is quickly exchanged with fury. Frustration boils inside him. He is too defenseless to intervene upon their enemy.

He peers back around to the grizzly sight and watches the murderer. He unrolls a large piece of paper from a pack and notes something on it, with a pencil. He then tucks his things away and heads straight north. Before the man disappears into the trees, he puts his weapon over his shoulder by its leather strap.

Joe is overcome with torment. He takes out his shank and squeezes the handle. From his crouched position beside the shack, he eyes the area of bushes that are still quivering from the killer having just pushed through them. He ponders his chances of successfully tracking their nemesis's trail right then and there and cleverly taking him down, but after serious consideration, concludes that he is incredibly outmatched under the circumstances, in every conceivable way. The powerlessness is excruciating. He waits a minute or two before tucking away his dagger and carefully making the short trip to Charlie's body. Part of him expects to be fired on from the bushes by the cunning killer, but that worry is forgotten when he arrives there within the murder scene. He winces at the sight of so much blood and his headless friend. Joe looks Charlie over from his crouch. "I'm sorry," he whispers. He indulges in deep thought for a moment to recall the good times shared with Charlie, even though they were brief, Joe appreciated their time together immensely. He maneuvers his way around the large, welling pool of blood and sets up at Charlie's feet. He quickly unties his shoe, removes them and takes up the trail set by his friends.

# 16

# J. Oskar Emmlington

J. Oskar Emmlington was born in the dead of winter, immediately after his identical twin brother Jakob into an aristocratic family and unto an adoring mother. It was Berlin, Germany, in 1942 and was during the height of Hitler and the third Reich's dominant reign. Down the street from the hospital, the Wannsee Conference had just approved plans for the 'Final Solution.' Oskar's father was an Englishman with dual citizenship, but his true heart was bound to Germany and his work there. He was a brilliant inventor and long-serving, adamant supporter of most of the Nazi Party's aspirations. He was coveted by them as not only a sub-contracted asset, but a friend. His illustrious affiliation was kept by great support from the Reich. At his request, he maintained strict anonymity while working as one of Heinrich Himmler's exclusive engineers for any and all things that he was approached with, for the war effort. His specialty was in prototypes. He invented many things of his own creation too all the while. The highly esteemed contributor would often times collaborate with other high-ranking engineers and scientists within the regime. The man would toil tirelessly in his endeavors and dealt well with the unrelenting roller coaster of failure and success.

In 1941, he was rumored to have had exclusive 'top-secret' appointment to aid in the S.S. and Gestapo chief Heinrich

Himmler's crackdown on the infamous Edelweiss Pirates. While most everything he did was strictly classified, this was different. Rather than the Reich using his genius to construct something tangible, this time they wanted him to help strategize a plan to eradicate the pirates. These 'particularly elusive irritants' as they were so previously dubbed by high ranking Nazi officials in the know, were becoming a downright subversion and the Nazis couldn't stand them. The pirates were a cultured, loosely organized youth group throughout Nazi Germany that defied the Nazi rule. They were the exact opposite of the compulsory 'Hitler Youth Movement.' They were a properly educated, self-sustaining, anti-authority, nonconforming thorn in the Reich's side and they were persistent in promoting and cultivating a free-thinking, resistant, and outrightly defiant German youth. As time wore on, from the middle of the 1930s to the early 1940s, the ever-growing pirates were hidden all over Nazi Germany, in plain sight and otherwise. They had even founded a secondary outlet, codenamed '*Navajos.*' Their mildly effective anti-Nazi field trips, where they would sing songs by bonfire had grown into strong-willed, successful campaigns to aid in the effort of many singular Nazi defectors, allied factions, and hunted Jews alike to escape the country. Oskar's mother was a native German and was also kept very secure within the Nazi Party, due to her birthright and who her father was. She was an unwavering loyalist from the beginning and her affiliation was also appreciated later by the third Reich. She spent most of the second world war as one of the country's top doctors specializing in brain surgeries, more specifically, lobotomies.

It was an extreme rarity in those days, given her gender, that a female could be a doctor, let alone one of such privilege within the medical community.

She was commanded by Reinhard Heydrich, who represented, *among other things*, the Reich's direct authority and endorsement to carry out such procedures and experiments for the greater good of the infamous 'Aryan race.' And she was happy to comply to the chief of the Reich's main security office or R.S.H.A. The woman was newly pregnant and had believed in the experiments so much that she had eagerly planned to work right up until her water broke, but the program was temporarily suspended following Reinhard's assassination by Czech assassins in June of 1942. After Heydrich's death and with her prestige at its peak, rumors began to circulate about her having unmediated involvement with S.S. captain Josef Mengele and many of his notorious experimental procedures at the Auschwitz camps in southwest Poland, though no official records were ever recovered, neither were there any records explaining her next three years.

In 1945 after Hitler's alleged suicide on the thirtieth of April, there is evidence to suggest that Oskar's mother was somehow able to gain safe passage with him to England. The details are unclear, but it had been long documented and confirmed that she had taken an infant with her when she fled. However, there was no mention as to why she had left with only one of her sons. Oskar's father was considered to have been killed when the unofficial fall of Nazi Germany was ushered in with the unrelenting shelling of Berlin by a Soviet led offensive. He resurfaced six years later, in 1951, in Texas, U.S.A. where under an ironclad alias, he had quickly become a successful oil tycoon. He was later credited in raising the bar on industry standards for having revitalized the crude oil refining process through a series of unprecedented mechanical and chemical design tweaks regarding various procedural efficiencies. He commuted unchecked between the U.S. and England for the next two decades.

By 1967, with their horrific past well behind them, his mother, who had spent her years in England partaking in *proper* brain surgeries, decided it was time to retire.

Oskar, after landing in England and experiencing years of varying detachment issues as a young child, to which could not particularly be explained by his parents or even the best doctors they could find, began attending boarding schools as to better integrate himself with others. As an adolescent he started to come out of his shell and rather than terrorizing neighborhood animals, set his focus on the revolving list of nannies that his mother would be forced to go through. He was jailed at the age of twenty-one for assault with a deadly weapon on his neighbor and animal cruelty for killing that same neighbor's dog. Both incidents occurred in the same altercation, to which it was unanimously agreed that he was the aggravated aggressor. It didn't come as a shock to his doting mother. Oskar had seen countless psychiatrists since the age of five. He was always thought of as incredibly erratic and wildly eccentric to his peers during his childhood. As he grew older, he left authority figures perplexed, because, though he was highly intelligent and considered a potential genius by all confirmed evaluations, he never applied himself. He would only find interests in things most considered peculiar.

By 1969, Oskar, with prison behind him and seemingly reformed, left his mother's side and moved to the United States, not to be with the absentee father that he despised or to work in his oil business that he had not a care for but to obtain an undergraduate degree and attend the university of Texas school of law, in Austin to earn a law degree. Oskar was not only ready to apply himself…but he wanted to. For him it wasn't about making his own money, it was about becoming something society could accept and recognize, furthermore; it was the one thing he knew he may need for himself in the future.

'A miraculous transformation,' his mother would say of the man he had become. By 1976, the year he got his last necessary degree, Oskar's father, who never seemed to do anything for his wife but line her bank accounts, was served divorce papers from her, citing irreconcilable differences due to physical abuse and numerous infidelities. Oskar was never bothered by the separation. He loathed his abusive father. If not for all the money he had given him through the years, he would have had no reason to ever associate with him at all.

In 1977, the year after Oskar got his degree and one month after his parent's divorce was finalized, his father was found drowned to death in his hot tub at his gargantuan Dallas estate. It was mere hours after he allegedly called the local pound to inquire about his missing Fox Terrier Fuchsl. His death was pronounced 'accidental drowning' due to acute alcohol poisoning.

Oskar was the sole proprietor of the will and his father's life insurance plan. As it turned out, he hated his son a little less than his ex-wife. He moved into his father's mansion shortly thereafter and he convinced his mother to join him from England soon after that. They enjoyed millions of dollars and lived a lavish lifestyle. Oskar even continued practicing law despite his lucrative inheritance and began specializing in high-profile homicide cases.

By 1981, Oskar, more curious than ever about his roots, his odd childhood memories, and his parents' checkered past, became fascinated with great historic wars. Where there was always an under-laying interest, these festering regards became obsessions. He lapped up all things military…with a particular soft spot for bygone militant eras. He was enthralled by weapons, artillery, uniforms, and everything in between. He had become infatuated with wartime history and studied all manner of accompanying societal construct and coinciding political paradigm as well as every type of world leader.

On the fringes of his extremely successful law firm and expensive, drunken celebratory dinners with colleagues in the field, Oskar read and researched obsessively day and night, and as his hobby grew, his passion for law and government and being a defense attorney altogether withered.

At the end of 1982, Oskar retired and decided to spend time and money having mansions built all over the globe, at some of his more favorite destinations. He embraces European designs and grows to appreciate antique works of art, so he furnishes his residences accordingly.

He exchanged drinking hard liquor with fine wines and appreciated smoking from a Calabash pipe.

It changed Oskar when his mother disclosed the secrets of her life and of his father's. Somehow in finally hearing it all, he had truly become himself and who he was meant to be. On the 23rd of December in 1983, Oskar's beloved mother died in her sleep of apparent natural causes. That would mark his last Christmas at the Dallas estate. Oskar put the mansion up for sale on the morning of December twenty-seventh and finalized its sale, effortlessly, on January third, 1984.

He took his second inheritance January sixth and traveled the world, where that spring, finally back in England, he met his future wife, a retired plant biologist and horticulturist.

They spend the subsequent three decades traveling the world hand-in-hand and staying at numerous extravagant places he had built. When not reading in one of their grand studies or working the land surrounding their properties, they pursue their common interest of aviation with regimented flying lessons. Other than coveted annual commitments of fine-dining with close friends, to which Oskar takes private flights alone to visit some of the members of his university alumni, former colleagues from his career in law and old friends from his time in the fossil fuels business, he and his wife are almost always together no matter where in the world they are, be it in America, Europe or elsewhere, having only the staff they keep as company. In recent years, their age has slowed them down considerably. Oskar's beloved wife has been splitting much of her time between reading and tending to the gardens and flowerbeds of their estates. Oskar has been spending *his* time further mastering a long-time passion… hunting.

# 17

# Know Your Enemy

Joe arrives about two-hundred-and-fifty yards northwest from where Charlie lay dead to a very-shaken pair of men within a small, clear area of the woods. Clive sits upon a boulder in front of a large, mauve-lilac bush. He hides within the potent aroma. Roebuck walks up to Joe, anticipating a grim report. Willy comes through the brush like a bolt of lightning.

"What the hell, Joe? What are we gonna do now, man?"

"Willy-boy, calm down!" urges Roe. Willy spits to the ground and wipes his mouth with his shirtsleeve.

"That crazy son of a bitch! Y'all see how he was dressed!!!" shouts Willy. "Whadda we do boys?"

"Willy, keep it down," says Roe.

"What'd you see, Joe?" asks Clive. Joe glances at all of the men. He slowly hands Roe Charlie's shoes. The big man receives them just as slow.

"When I heard that third shot, I wasn't sure if it was for Charlie, for you or for us," imparts Roebuck.

"He finished Charlie off," confirms Joe. "He was alone and headed north from the east." Joe pauses a moment before proceeding. "After each kill, he disappears for a while, not to be seen, or heard from."

"What do you make of it?" asks Roe.

"Can't be certain, but it seems he takes us one at a time by choice. One encounter at a time."

"Are you serious, man?" says Willy frantically.

"What? Wait, if that's what he's doing, we can change our game plan," suggests Clive.

"I think we should," returns Joe, promptly.

"As he was walking up to Charlie to… Y'know, while you were all running down here, he fired up into the air. He was lookin' right at me, as if to back me up and scare me off. Now I'm sure if threatened, he'd…"

"Oh my God," exclaims Clive, inadvertently interrupting Joe in the process.

Willy begins to curse, "That motherfuckin' prick! That yellow-bellied bastard!"

"He's playing with us!" adds Clive.

"Joe!" he calls. "You know what we gotta do? *NOW*!"

"What are you thinkin'?" inquires Joe.

"We all gotta get movin' *right* now! While we have time to make up good ground."

"We should also move by night," adds Roe, while bending down to un-wrap his feet. Clive continues…

"If this sick son of a bitch is only huntin' us one by one, then he's already got his man, rest his soul and we've got a while to *really* move…right?"

"Right," answers Joe, in reassurance. "But we don't know for sure that's what this guy's doing, or if he is, for how long and we wouldn't wanna entice him into to trying to take one of us out simply because we've made our presence convenient. Look, he's moving north, and obviously going somewhere! So, we go north too, till sunrise… But we *must* maintain awareness at all times."

Clive hops down from his rock, with renewed vigor.

"Un-fuckin' believable!" exclaims Willy, as he paces.

"These are small, but'll do jus' fine," says Roebuck of the shoes.

The four men stand in a circle. They gather their wits and align their energies.

"Okay fellas…north," says Clive. The men search each other's faces. There is a shared determination in their eyes.

"Straight north," says Roebuck. Joe nods and interjects. "Remember boys, as far as we can tell right now, that fucker was also moving north, but he entered the heavier woods to my right, so we'll need to mind the immediate east too for a while and if we are forced to divert from north-bound at all, ideally it should be northwest. Obviously, things can change in an instant, but let's hope for the best."

As the men start out, Joe smacks Willy on the back of his shoulder.

"The motherfucker," says Willy, of Charlie's killer. "I pray that prick went north for a reason, man, if he shows us where he's come from, he's fucking finished."

The men tread carefully. Any mistakes could be fatal, more now than ever. They hope their gamble is a wise one.

They are tired but venture on with a chip on their shoulder and rejuvenated motivation.

The foursome walk for hours and keep their rare conversations as positive and productive as possible, if one of them slightly cracks and makes mention of their dismal reality, the others are supportive, and are inspirational as they aspire to restore a positive outlook. Among them, Willy is the most talkative. One minute he is telling a well-received joke and viciously cursing their pursuer the next. They press on through the forest until the afternoon, stopping only to drink from puddles or when they must help each other through the obstacles of the forest.

"A big, fat, frustrating, fucking un-ending maze!" exclaims Willy as they enter a thinner, less-complex part of the wilds.

"Was that *three F*s Willy?" asks Clive in a playful manner.

"Huh? Well, let me see… Fat, frustrated…fucking. Yeah, I suppose it was! No, wait… Wouldn't it be three sets of 'PHs'?"

Clive laughs. "I'm not sure who's joke was worse, mine or yours."

"Yours man, you started it." Before Clive can respond Willy shouts out. "Damn fellas! Ya'll see that?" he blurts as he points on ahead in the distance. "There, up yonder!"

"What is it?" asks Roe.

"There, Rowboat! Way up there," he replies, still pointing with his grubby index finger.

Clive and Roe look up the way, to no avail.

Joe, a short distance in front of the group, has spotted it too, "I see it."

"What the hell is it?" Willy asks.

Roebuck squints his eyes. "It looks like a big heap a' scrap metal."

"Ahhh… I see it now," says Clive. "What *is* that?"

"It's an old, wrecked spaceship that we're gonna fix up and use to fly on outta here," says Roe as they draw near.

The men reach the large pile of metal to find that what they had located from afar was a long abandoned Divco milk truck, circa 1946. The boxy vehicle has no plates and its front doors are ajar.

"Holy shit boys!" Willy says excitably, as he sticks his head inside one of the vehicles' few windows. He tries the sliding side door just behind the driver's side. It is corroded shut.

"Y'all thinkin' what I'm thinkin'?" asks Roe.

"I'm thinkin', time for some dinner," replies Willy as he carefully sets his sack down on the curved hood of the washed-out vehicle. The truck's white paint long turned cream color and the decorative, curved red and blue lines sheens are sullied. The luster had left gradually through the many years.

"You're not thinking it will *start,* are ya Rowboat?" says Clive sarcastically.

"Ha-ha, very funny."

"Roe's thinkin' we must be gettin' close to civilization," affirms Joe as they surround the truck and look it over.

"Bingo!" says Roebuck, pointing to Joe. The big man tries opening the sliding door on the right side of the truck. Like the other slider, it too won't budge. He takes a seat in the passenger side of the vehicle's cab. There isn't much to see. He fidgets with the glove compartment.

"It's a good sign," says Willy as he pokes around his bag and shoves a piece of meat into his mouth.

"It's a *great* sign," adds Joe. "Hey, this glove box is stuck, we oughta pry it open," says Roe.

"You are honestly not afraid of catching something from that carcass, are you?" says Clive.

"I am honestly not," replies Willy, proudly. He takes a moment to chew and swallow. "What choice I got? Should I start eating plants I know nothing about? Grass? It's simple, y'all can starve to death if you want, but I been taking a few small chunks of this here bunny now and then, *just enough of it* and I feel fine so far. So long as I don't take a critical bullet, I'll stay alive to the end because of this here shit," he says as he wipes his hands on his shirt. "Like I said, you all can drop like flies if y'all want and the ones of you who've been good to me, I may not eat."

"May not, huh," says Clive. Willy laughs and lightly punches his friend on the arm. Roe makes his way into the back of the truck through the door in the center of the cab's partition wall.

"We haven't eaten for days, and if I actually focused on my hunger, I would likely feel weaker from it than I ever have in my whole life, But this bag 'a yours, I don't know man, rotting, old rabbit flesh that you found might not be the answer we're lookin' for," says Joe. He poses a question for Willy to ponder. "Like, what if you've contracted something from it, but it just hasn't hit you yet. Could you imagine battling food poisoning out here on top of everything else?"

"A rabbit doesn't just die of natural causes," says Clive.

"Well, you can all suit yourselves… And a' course a rabbit can die of natural causes. But what difference does it make?" says Willy as he stuffs a little more meat into his cheek, as if it were chewing tobacco.

He closes his sack, walks around the front of the truck, and slumps down onto the driver's seat. He begins searching all around the cab of the truck; Joe and Clive enter the passenger side and carry on through to join Roebuck in the back. Willy is delighted to find a dirty, dusty, gray fedora under the passenger side seat.

"Hey! Hey! Fits great," he says loudly, with his cheek bulging, as he exits the vehicle. He lays down, pulls himself under the truck through the grass and proceeds to look around underneath.

Other than just dirt and grime, the guys in the back find a few cloth bags with illegible, soggy papers, soiled trash, and a bag of seven-inch aluminum gutter spikes being the highlight.

Joe and Clive each take some and put them in their pockets. Roe declines, as he has nowhere to put them. The men return to the front of the truck. Clive hops back outside.

"Hey boys, we gotta get into the glove box. It's either locked or fused shut," says Roebuck. He and Joe sit in the front and go to work on the glove compartment, while Clive starts in on popping the hood. Willy appears out from under the truck.

"Nice hat," says Roe.

"Hey, thanks Rowboat. Almost as nice as your jammy-jams," returns Willy. Roe chuckles and shakes his head.

"Hey Roe, what *is* up with the outfit?" asks Clive from the front of the truck.

"Now, now boys, let's just all stay focused on the tasks at hand," replies Roe from behind the steering wheel... "I suppose not all of us had the luxury of being abducted while fast asleep and cozy in their bed."

The men share in a short moment of laughter. Roe tries not to allow it, but his smile slips as he stares through the cracked windshield and off into the wilderness.

After a few minutes, the hood job seems futile for Clive. Willy leans beside Joe on the passenger side doorframe. Joe hands him over some spikes.

"Nice," says Willy as he looks them over and shoves them in his back pocket.

"See, with this here nail," says Joe, "I can...wedge it in the crack; but she won't budge." He struggles with the glove compartment latch.

"Here... Let's give that a whack while you hold that nail right in place," suggests Willy. "Just one minute. Let me find something to hammer on it with."

Willy takes a walk around the truck. He nods at Clive, who is leaned on its hood. He tugs his hat brim down slightly and follows around the brim with his finger and thumb, displaying a great big smile. "Dapper now, huh Clive?"

Clive looks at him as if he might be crazy and smiles in amusement. Willy finds a sizeable rock and leans back inside. "Okay Joe, you ready?"

"Go get it," he says, as he stabilizes the long nail.

After a couple firm whacks, the compartment pops open. A few things fall to the floor, along with the rock. The door dangles at Joe's knees.

"Any gold?" asks Willy, as he digs in. Clive looks on through the windshield.

"A map would be nice," replies Joe.

"Yeah really, agrees Roebuck… I keep thinking of how hard it is out here. All we'd need is a cellphone or something… Just turn it on, flip on a map, and from right where we stand, we could walk in a beeline straight to a road. It's so messed up."

After a few moments of Willy mumbling to himself and sifting through the small mess at Joe's feet, he lets out an exuberant shout. "Holy shit!" Willy then pushes himself back through the passenger side window and runs past Clive, bumping him as he goes. He skips and cheers as he dances beside the truck.

"Whoa, whoa," calls Roe. "What do you got?" He and Joe exit the milk truck.

"What did you find?" asks Clive.

Willy settles down and walks toward the men.

He holds both his hands out. "One on top of the other." The men, now all staring at him, wait attentively for the reveal.

Willy slowly takes his top hand away to uncover a small tin with a Houston Oilers emblem on it.

"Geez Willy, I know they ain't a football team no more 'n all, but this is too much," says Roe.

"No, no, Boat, look!" says Willy as he opens the tin to uncover about two dozen or more well-preserved, wooden, strike-anywhere matches.

"Oh, my God," whispers Joe.

"We need to have a fire boys. We have to!" cries Clive.

"I'll eat some goddamn strange rabbit once it's cooked!" The men, still in shock by the find and the potential of it, say nothing as they turn to Clive; Willy fishes around in his pockets.

"Wait, just wait," says Joe. "Let's think about what this can mean."

"Warmth and food! Think about it, Joe," urges Clive.

"I just hope they work fellas," says Roe.

Willy takes out a flattened pack of mangled Lucky Strike cigarettes from his jeans pocket, ignites a match with a 'pop' from alongside the truck's hood, and lights one up.

Clive cries out with glee, "That answer your question Rowboat?" The man can barely contain his excitement.

The trio looks upon Willy in bewildered fascination as he deeply inhales and exhales a steady stream of blue-gray smoke.

"Y'all want one?" he asks as he takes another drag, demonstrating pure ecstasy. He holds them outward.

"I quit sixteen years ago," says Roebuck as he lumbers forward and grabs one out of Willy's out-stretched pack.

"First time for everything," says Clive, taking one for himself.

Joe then reaches and sifts through the pack, half of them are broken, he finds one that's in good shape and puts it between his lips. "I quit, after a pulmonary issue, not too long ago."

Roe and Clive look over at Joe with concern. Willy has his eyes closed as he takes another powerful pull on his cigarette. The tip lights up bright orange. He tilts his head back and holds the smoke inside. "That was one of the best things I had goin' back home, y'know, being able to abstain... Fuck it." adds, Joe with a grin.

"Normally, I'd try to talk you out of it," says Willy, with eyes still closed as he exhales.

The four men stand in a circle, each one smoking his cigarette in a rare moment of complete, uncontested serenity.

"So, we gonna have us a fire tonight or what?" inquires Clive.

"Let's not think about anything right now," says Roe.

The friends stand in silence. For the moment, in the forest, peace is all there is.

# 18

# A Tiny Light Amidst Infinite Dark

Dusk has crept in and surrounded the milk truck. "Maybe we could use some of the old fabric from the truck," says Clive.

"Well, we could, I suppose," replies Roe.

"I got something," Joe says, as he reaches to his pockets and produces two wads of paper. "I tore this out of a book in my shed. I figured," Joe picks up a decent-sized branch from the ground. "Ya never know."

"Amazing! So, what's the plan again then?" inquires Clive.

"Well, we're gonna crash in the truck. It should provide good cover, then we'll sit awhile by the fire. Those who wanna eat, will eat," says Joe.

Roe nods. "Then, we'll head out," he adds.

"Yeah, if we wanna take advantage, we'll have to move well once night falls. We cover as much ground as possible, we'll need our rest, so at dawn's break, we sleep. Taking shifts, keeping watch. There'll be no more moving during the day. This coward wants to hunt us, good luck finding us in the dark... And what better way to find civilization than at night, when the lights are on," affirms Joe.

The three gather deadwood till their arms are at capacity. When they arrive at the milk truck, they're greeted by Willy, who has been busy stuffing rocks underneath the wrecked vehicle. "Hey," he says, enthusiastically, as they drop the wood beside him. With a bent smoke hanging from his lips, he begins cramming the lumber beneath. Joe and Roebuck pry the rear doors open. It is relatively spacious. There are no windows in the back of the delivery truck other than in the rear doors. A perfect place to rest before the long night that lies ahead of them.

Inside the front Clive closes and locks the door that divides the cab and box of the truck. He then steps outside and pushes on the front doors of the truck's cab one after the other. Their partially seized hinges somewhat resist the action and while the doors won't latch completely closed, they are at least set in tight against their frames.

The men climb into the back and settle in. When all four are inside, Joe and Roebuck proceed to pull the back doors *nearly* shut, purposely leaving them open a crack, so they can monitor the outside area. The group aspire to get comfortable. Willy dutifully offers out some of his infamous cherries.

It's not quite time to sleep, so the men indulge in conversation. The talks are small and mundane at first, until Willy speaks. "Why do you think we're all here? Like…why *us*?"

The men look at one another. Roebuck reluctantly shrugs his shoulders.

"I'm sure we've all been trying to figure that out," affirms Joe. Clive nods in agreement. He stares a hole into the truck's floor, as Joe voices his thoughts on the matter. "We haven't exactly had time to sit down and analyze all of the possibilities."

Moments pass and no one says a word.

Soon, the men talk of their backgrounds and consider any possible connections they may share pertaining to why they were brought to the forest. They come up what seem like idle coincidences and nothing remotely telling.

They are increasingly dumbfounded…and their shared anger grows. Roebuck tries to alleviate their collective frustration. "At least we have each other and we're not alone. I mean…as fucked up as this is, that'd be even worse."

"Awe Rowboat, that's hella sweet," says Willy. "You know what would *really* suck?" He quickly answers his own question. "If we were all a bunch of assholes."

A silent moment passes, while the group regains its composure. "Who's got first watch?" asks Clive.

"I'll take her," volunteers Roe.

"I have a feeling we can all sleep at the same time in here," suggests Joe.

"I can go for that," says Willy. "If that son of a bitch wants to take us in our sleep, so be it. Better off not seeing it coming… Huh Joe?" adds Willy from underneath the fedora that is now propped on his face where he lays. Joe recalls how Charlie had said something eerily similar the day before he was murdered.

"Well, I'm gonna stay awake and keep watch awhile *anyways*," says Roe.

Joe and Clive follow Willy's lead and lay down.

"Hey, Rowboat… I like your P.J.s," whispers Willy.

It isn't long before the three men in the back of the truck are snoring away, with Roe propped up on his knees, staring blankly through the crack in the doors. A rare glimpse of emotional turmoil is prominently etched into his expression, as he peers through the forest and way beyond. The big man's blue eyes well up and when he looks to the darkening sky a single tear falls from each.

Hours later, the night is pitch black, and the other men are still laid out and fast asleep. Roe shakes Joe awake first.

"It's time," he says. Joe shakes Clive and Clive shakes Willy.

"Holy shit!" exclaims the last man to wake up. He adjusts his hat and pulls himself to his knees. "It's fuckin' freezing tonight."

Outside, the men work efficiently. Willy disperses the wood to Joe and the rock to Clive, which they pass to Roe who in turn allocates the wood into a pile and the rock into a circular formation around it. When the pit is assembled, Joe stuffs the spaces between the branches with his shreds of *Mein Kampf*. Willy approaches with four cigarettes in his mouth, and after the first two matches prove to be duds, he mumbles, "Oh, don't you dare." But third time's a charm. He successfully lights all four and doles them out to his friends. He proceeds to ignite the fire cautiously with the same burning match.

The men sit around it in a circle. "She's a beauty, boys!" states Clive, whole-heartedly.

"Yessir!" says Roe as he flicks his butt into the fire.

"Alright Joe," says Willy.

"What's alright?"

"Y'know… Do the honors," he says as he attempts to pass the bag of food around the fire to Joe.

Joe returns a suspecting look back to Willy. "No, no, you go on and do it," he replies.

Willy applies some greasy chunks of rabbit meat onto a thin, wooden, wet branch; he holds the skewer outward and begins to carefully sear the meat.

"Geez, y'all know what's givin' me the creeps?" says Roe. "I don't even know the date today… And here we are, set in the damn Bermuda triangle of forests."

"Yeah," adds Joe. "We can't be sure of much, can we?"

"That coward!" says Willy, in instant anger. "Bringin' us out here and fuckin' with us! What I wouldn't give to fuck him up! Fuck!" he shouts as he burns his fingers on a chunk of cooked meat. The men pass the skewer around, each carefully tearing off a piece in turn, until it arrives at Joe, he passes on the opportunity and is especially surprised that Clive had taken a piece.

"Goddamn, y'know fellas, if this psycho could see the light and did track us…we'd sure be easy pickins'!" Willy says nonchalantly. They stare at each other around the pit, all feeling incredibly vulnerable. "Or what if this fucker does hunt at night? Y'know, with like…night vision goggles or some shit? Then, we're fucked for sure!" The men stare at Willy. "Awe man, sorry boys. This meat has instantly given me some serious fuckin' energy fellas," he adds.

"Y'all ever think about huntin' some game of our own? I mean, we got matches, no real proper way to clean anything, but a fresh animal, clean or not, could *really* help us here," suggests Roe.

Clive perks up. "I hear ya, Roe. Lord knows I've been thinkin' about that all along. But… I don't know…if we start makin' ourselves at home in here…it'd likely increase our chances of being susceptible to that maniac's attack. I realize we're starving. It sure does hurt physically and it can mess with one mentally, but… I just don't know. It's so confusing…we could just, come out of the woods to a road and it's all over. I guess it's that, that keeps me going and yet at the same time, it's serving as a distraction."

"We can't get all...'*Lord of the Flies*' out here and start settin' down roots. Our focus should just be movin' on out. Fuck this forest," says Willy. They share a few more skewers of scorched meat before gearing up for their night's venture. It is difficult to leave the comforts of the fire, but the men have little choice.

"I just keep daydreaming that if we walk enough in one direction, we'll hit a highway, ya know? Or a back road even," says Joe. "How could we not?"

"Maybe we'll run into some more men," suggests Willy as he stomps out the remaining embers.

"Alright, boys, let's go get 'em," inspires Roebuck. With that, they slowly slip into the darkness. The stars slowly reveal themselves and surround the moon as the sounds of a coyote's howls bellow throughout the cool wilderness. The men keep relatively close together as they go.

"Hey," whispers Willy. "What do you all make of the matches?"

"What do you mean?" asks Clive.

"Well, 'Houston Oilers,' now we ain't *in* Houston?"

"No... I'd say not."

"And what's with this cold temperature and all that rain? Anyway, that truck...no plates or nothin'...but she was definitely forties. But them matches ain't that old... Someone put them there. Maybe the killer?"

"Maybe a prisoner," quips Joe.

"Where the hell you think we are in the world, Joe?"

"I dunno...north...a northern state somewhere would be my guess, maybe New York? Looks like my neck of the woods... But who can really say for certain, we're no experts."

"You know what? What we oughta do?" announces Willy. "We oughta burn this fuckin' forest down. The whole goddamn place! Then someone would see it fellas. See the fire from afar, from the sky. Come and investigate."

"The forest is so green and still pretty damp from the rain," says Clive.

"I'm not sure there's enough matches to create a fire of the magnitude Willy-boy is talkin' about." Roe ponders as he walks. "Coulda' lit the milk truck, that'd burn awhile…a good ol' toxic fire with that awful, black smoke."

"Fuck!" exclaims Willy. "We should have done that!"

"Better during the day if we were going to," suggests Roe.

"Hold up, everybody just wait a minute," says Joe. He stops and so do the others. "Is this something we should seriously consider? Because if it is, we shouldn't take another step northward. We should try and make our way back, whether we find the truck in the dark or not, at least we aren't wasting energy. We sleep and at dawn we light it up. The question is, is it really worth the effort? I would hope it couldn't hurt but, where I'm from when you see a smoke stack raising up from a field, you don't think much of it and you carry on with your day, I just worry the only person's interest we will attract is you know who's and therein lies another gamble. Perhaps we draw him to it and we're long gone, but what if we're not, what if it just pulls him closer to us."

The men stand in the dark and weigh their options.

"It'd have been much easier to decide if we were still with the truck," says Roe.

"How did we not think of this earlier?" adds Clive.

"We were high on food and smoke," says Willy.

"I say fuck waiting, fuck going back… Y'know what we could do?" says Joe. "We could continue on and if and when we come across another one of those buildings, we decide then, whether to light the fucker up or not." The others like that idea.

The men carry on for hours through the frigid night and all kinds of obstacles. The forest is alive with things unseen. The dark provides better cover from their pursuer, but not much else. The group's frustrations escalate.

"Man, I can't feel my feet, they're ice blocks," says Willy.

"Yeah, be quiet Willy! At least you got some real clothes on. I'm wearin' a thin layer of polyester over here," snaps Roe.

"Hope ya'll are immune to poison ivy like I am 'cause not a one of us is gon' see it coming," professes Willy to the group.

"Where the fuck are we?" exclaims Clive. "We've been at this all night and for days!" he says loudly. He stops dead in his tracks. "It's like we're in hell!"

"Easy now, we'll get there Clive," says Joe in an encouraging tone.

"I mean, have you ever seen anything like it in your entire life? We could *try* to get lost and not do a better job, Joe!" says Clive.

"I know man, I know. We'll get there, we've got to!"

"I'm sorry guys, but it's too much! We need to stop. I'm fucking starving and I think that rabbit's fucking with my guts. We need to take a rest. I've gotten all sliced up through the bush. We're all freezing… Let's just… Let's just stop for a while. Morning can't be too far off now any-damn-way."

"Okay Clive," says Joe.

"Sounds good to me," says Willy. "Let's find us a good spot."

"It's just…"

"It's okay," says Roe. "We all feel it," he says, in an attempt to calm Clive.

The men press on for a short time until they discover a small valley within the forest to settle down into.

"When dawn breaks," says Joe, "this will provide good cover." Despite being tired and cold, the men do their best to get comfortable and bed down.

Willy offers out some cherries to his friends. "I've been swallowing 'em whole…like pills… Takes longer to digest that way."

"Pits and all?" asks Roe.

"Yes sir," replies Willy. "Seems to keep me a little fuller…a little longer."

Willy gets to Joe and offers him a handful. "No thanks Willy-boy," he says. Willy winks, nods, and smacks him on the back. The men whisper a little while about the plan once daylight comes.

As soon as all is quiet for an extended period of time, Joe speaks up. "I got first watch."

# 19

# Above the Hollow

Rays of sunshine blaze down through the forest in beams. Ash, elm, birch, and countless others surround the valley. All the men are asleep within it. Willy wakes up quick, with a gasp. "Shit!" he whispers, as he had fallen asleep during his watch. "Fuck me!" he says as he fumbles to light a bent, cracked cigarette. He shuffles through the tin, taking careful inventory of the remaining matches with his filthy thumb. He leans his back on the damp earth of the valley wall and scans the area while he sets there and smokes. The group's chosen place of refuge appears more crater than valley. It is about ten feet deep with a diameter of around forty feet. It is filled with dirt, grass, brush, moss, and rock. He looks up at the towering trees.

Birds chirp from all over as they bask in the early morning sunlight's arrival. It is a setting so tranquil for the dwellers of the forest, all but the men, who have been through so much suffering within it.

Willy scratches a series of itchy insect bites on his arm and looks closely at his friends. Joe is laying on his side. His head resting on a mound of dirt, hugging it as if it were his pillow from home. Clive is in the fetal position, his upper body sheltered by the bush he's crawled under.

And Roe sleeps leaning his back to a boulder. The three men look like death to Willy.

Dirty, malnourished, and pale.

"Motherfucker," mutters Willy under his breath as he observes his friends. Suddenly he feels something on his thigh and slowly looks down. A bull snake has decided to slither over his right leg and then underneath his left, on it's way back onto the valley wall. Willy's skin crawls. He stays completely still, holds his breath, and watches the snake disappear behind some rocks. He flicks his cigarette butt and springs up onto his feet. He wakes Roe up first.

"Mornin' Willy-boy," he says as he rubs his eyes with grimy fists. "What say you give me one of those dirty smokes, partner?"

Willy takes out the pack. "Here ya go, Rowboat... Not too many left," Willy says as he hands one over. He continues on to get Clive up.

With a big inhale, then exhale, Clive crawls out from under the bush.

He walks over to Joe. "Up and at 'em," he says, kneeling down and jostling Joe's shoulder.

"Anything interesting on last watch?" he asks as he comes to.

Willy stands up. "Uhh, nah... Same shit, different night," he replies, rather quickly.

"I see... Well, no news is good news," says Joe.

"I heard that." The men sit and talk quietly about whether staying put within the valley is a viable strategy for the day or not.

"This place may save our lives," suggests Joe.

"This is a tough one. I know the plan was to travel by night, but at the same time, if we're found out down here, we'd be easy pickins'," says Roebuck.

"If this freak only takes one of us at a time, though," adds Clive, "then it should be all the same, whether we're in this hole or not."

"The only real differences," says Joe, "are that we have a better chance of preserving ourselves down here 'til nightfall, and at least down *here*, we'd have a greater chance of hearing him coming too…maybe we could even get the drop on him."

"Whichever three of us are lucky enough to survive," interjects Willy.

"Yeah, that's right," says Joe, in a slightly condescending tone. "The lucky ones might just get a run at him, Willy!"

"Oh, I like that very much. That sounds *very* interesting," replies Willy, with a crooked grin.

"Well, we seem to be at an impasse boys," says Roe, dutifully inserting himself back into the debate.

"We should simply put it to a vote then," advises Joe.

"Y'all know what? Damn it all, I say stay…till twilight time, fellas, that's my vote," says Roe. "To hell with it."

"Ya know, this plan will work," adds Joe. "We just need to see it through." He nods at Roebuck.

"Democracy, huh? What happens in the event of a tie?" inquires Willy.

"We'll cross that bridge when we get there," answers Joe.

"I'm gonna hav' to say go," asserts Clive. "Waitin' here all day just for another night walk doesn't interest me at all."

They look to Willy. He smiles. "I'm gonna need a bit to mull this one over, marinade it, if you will," he says.

Clive puts his head in his hands.

"So, what do y'all do, in the real world?" asks Willy. "I know Rowboat's a mover, self-employed, but whadda' you two do?"

"I am also self-employed," answers Joe. "I have a small residential building company."

"I work at a sports equipment store and dabble in coaching hockey," says Clive fondly.

"Hockey, huh?"

"I've told you this Willy."

"Suppose I'm just buying time."

"Vote Willy," says Roe. "Geez Joe, I sure would like to know a guy like you back home… I done lots of building, and I'm lookin' for a job, somethin' awful. Too bad we're from different ends of the goddamn country," he says. "What's your specialty?"

"Carpentry," returns Joe, "but I can just about do everything when it comes to building construction."

"I'll be damned!" exclaims Willy. "Yes sir! We sure could be a pair, I'd fuckin' haul ass, straight to New York too, once we escape this bullshit."

"I'll hold you to it," says Joe as he points to Willy.

"Now, Willy-boy!" calls Roe. "What's my little old moving company, chopped liver?"

"Rowboat, I'd love me some liftin' 'n all, it's just I couldn't work alongside a man who wears his pajamas outside the house!"

Roe laughs.

"So, Willy, how about that vote?" urges Clive.

"Well, sir! It seems that if I vote stay, we stay. But if I vote go, we are tied…like I said what then?"

"We draw twigs," quips Joe quickly with a stare that displays his impatience.

"Oh, that sounds fun. I vote go!"

Now wondering if Willy cares at all about a plan, Joe collects four twigs. "Okay, *here*'s how it'll work," he says.

"Willy and Clive are the team representing the 'go' side. Roe and I represent the 'stay' side. Whoever draws the shortest twig between Boat and Clive wins! And we will thereby follow the winner's originally submitted *democratic* vote." Joe looks at Clive.

"Why ain't I gettin' a pull?" interjects Willy.

"Because you don't," says Roe.

"Oh, well fine, no sense in delayin' the inevitable, pull twigs!"

Joe, Clive, and Roe give each other a look. Willy rubs his hands together, in anticipation of the outcome, and stares at the twigs in Joe's clenched fist. Before the two men can 'draw straws,' the group hear the sounds of snapping above. They scramble for cover. Joe puts his finger to his lips. Everyone is silent.

Joe, Clive, and Willy take refuge at the base of the dirt wall closest to the side where the noise came from, while Roe is more to the center of the valley, behind the boulder he had slept against. The noise gets louder and more prominent as they wait.

The men look like they've seen a ghost, and the snapping and rustling noises sound more and more like calculated footsteps as they get closer.

Joe holds his breath. He imagines the man he'd seen before in some grand old uniform, clutching his infamous gold-plated West German C.E.T.M.E. Assault Jäger rifle, model fifty-eight. It is hard for the men to keep still as their adrenaline soars. The sound travels gradually southwest of their east point position, and as it does, Joe exhales slowly and begins to climb the short cliff of the crater wall and toward its rim.

"No Joe, no!" whispers Clive, who firmly grasps his shirtsleeve. Joe ignores the protest. Clive lets go. He ascends up, the ten feet to ground's main level and he slowly peeks over the grass. "I don't believe it," he says, under his breath. He raises his head a little more to see the beautiful doe in its entirety.

"Is it you?" he whispers. Joe calls out, "It's okay! It's a deer."

The men below expel giant gasps as they exhale, in relief of the news.

"Unbelievable," says Willy as he turns and shakes Clive, who is clearly in an odd state of shock and relief.

"We've gotta hunt it!" adds Willy.

"Let me get a look," Roe says as he lumbers from his rock and up, alongside Joe. The two men watch the doe until in no time at all, she bounds off south through the trees.

"Thought we were done for," laughs Roe as he gives his buddy a shove with his shoulder.

"Yeah," replies Joe. He takes a deep breath and releases it. They stare out into the forest in silence for a moment to the area the deer had disappeared into, before sliding back down the dirt wall. "Well, now who's pullin' again?" asks Willy.

"I'll be changing my vote," says Joe. The men share a good laugh, though it is a shaky one.

They smoke two cigarettes between them before resuming their journey north. They travel very quietly and carefully and stay low. The men seem even more wary of their stalker after the false alarm they received in the hollow. Clive stops and motions everyone to come to him.

"I hear running water," he says. "We gotta find the source and drink." The men agree and pan out to find the water. Joe finds it first and waves his dagger in the air to signal his friends.

They join him at narrow stream. As the four proceed to drink, Joe stops. "It's flowing south," he says.

"What of it?" asks Roebuck.

Joe reflects for a moment… "Nothin'," he replies.

"This hunger boys, it's…it's taking its toll… I'm grateful for these streams and puddles but, we need more, we need nutrients…with every passing hour I feel weaker," says Clive. Once sufficiently hydrated, he fills his coke bottle about three quarters full, stuffs a new leaf into the open end, and puts it in its place in his back pocket.

They trudge through the woods with slow yet gradual progress. They are tired, but still advance well. However fatigued, their efficiency grows the longer they are together, and they keep their actions as calculated and supported as possible, when need be. The afternoon sun beats down on them, and they decide to take refuge in a low-lying, heavily overgrown area.

"There're tall trees and plenty of thorns here…this'll be a good spot, for now," declares Joe.

"I can't believe how hot it is during the day and how cold it is at night," says Roebuck. The men agree.

"We'll continue on as soon as dusk comes. We have no choice, if we wanna rest *now*," adds Joe.

"I'm just gonna hope for a clear night tonight with plenty of stars and moonlight," says Clive. "So we can see what we're doing out there at least a little bit."

The men finally, painstakingly give in to their hunger and eat some of Willy's cherries after Clive carefully rinses them off with what little water he has in his glass bottle. They then smoke the last of his cigarettes. "A sad end," proclaims Willy as he flicks the last butt.

"Feels like more rain," says Joe of the moisture in the air. Soon after, and with Roe taking first watch, all is silent.

# 20

# The Storm

It was still Roebuck's watch when it started. The wind gradually picked up and steadily escalated to a force that blustered through the woods ferociously. Trees swayed and thrashed as thunder and lightning began to take control of the sky, which grumbled again, ready to unleash its fury. *Should I wake them?* Roe wonders to himself. *They'll wake when the rain arrives, if not by the sound of thunder,* he concludes. Before long, the rain indeed does come and the thunder rolls ever closer. Lightning flashes across the sky as the rainfall increases from steady to torrential. Joe wakes first, with Clive and Willy waking immediately after. The men are in the middle of a full-fledged thunderstorm. The forest is loud and lights up bright and often.

"What the fuck!" yells Willy holding his hat to his head; and as the sky lights up again. Water is running steadily off the center of his hat's brim and nose.

"Let's go!" yells Roe. "We gotta find better cover! Go boys! Go!" shouts Clive.

The men scurry in the darkness. White, strobing light comes in pulses and illuminates their path as they scramble to find suitable shelter.

The rain pours relentlessly with no sign of letting up. The men are drenched and muddy. Just when it seems there's no place to hide, Joe cries out, "I don't believe it! Look! Straight ahead!"

"What?" calls Clive over the noise of the storm.

"Follow me!" persists Joe as a flash of light momentarily reveals a shack.

They run through the woods for twenty yards or so. The men lose and gain sight of the building many times on their way. Finally, they arrive in front of it and run right in without hesitation. This one has a door. Joe jumps into it with his shoulder, falling and landing hard as the door flies opens with a crash. The men file in. Roe slams it shut and quickly barricades it with a dresser. Rain is running in through countless openings in the roof and along the walls. The structure shudders within the strong wind.

Dripping wet and unable to see much, they fight to catch their breaths. Willy drops his bag and wrings out the bottom of his shirt.

"Well, if anyone was here, they're gone now," says Roe.

"Fuck!" shouts Willy. "This is bullshit! We can't go any further tonight."

"Not in this," says Clive.

"We aren't goin' nowhere tonight. No pullin' twigs, no nothin'," stamps Roebuck.

"You got the matches, Willy?"

"Let's see what's in here, if they're not ruined," says Joe.

After drying his hands, checking his pockets and investigating the tin case, Willy begins to thrash around. "Fuck!" he yells and throws the tin and then whatever else he can get his hands on inside the shack.

"The tips, they're fuckin' mush!" he shouts.

"Alright, alright!" says Roe with authority. "Relax Willy-boy, relax. That kind of behavin' ain't gonna get us anywhere."

"We're all gonna wait inside here and let this pass," says Joe. "We're not going anywhere tonight. So, let's just be happy we're sheltered, hopefully we'll even dry out some," he adds.

"We won't dry out for a week," blurts Willy in frustration.

"Get it together, Willy!" snaps Roebuck.

"Let's all just calm down," says Clive.

Once the group pull themselves together, they unanimously decide that there is no need for a watchman. Soon, within the chaos and without much choice in the matter, the men are fast asleep. The storm pounds the woods and the structure for hours. It fills waterways, wipes away weak foliage, and brings down feeble trees and branches. Just one of nature's ways of rejuvenating the forest and replenishing it.

Joe awakens and sits up on the floor of the shack to a much milder atmosphere. The sun is barely hung above the trees, as it slowly rises. It's breezy and drizzling within the warmer air. He cracks the door open against its barricade and looks outside. There are disheveled remnants of obvious destruction strewn about. He grabs at his damp clothing and looks down at his hands. They are cleaner than they have been in days and his fingertips are pruned. His stomach rumbles, prompting him to put a wrinkled hand against it. It feels sunken-in and his attention to it makes it feel even worse, as it abruptly sounds off again. Joe looks around the interior of the shelter and studies his friends. Roe and Willy are each on a bed, while Clive is on the floor. Their dirty clothes are torn, there are leaves stuck to parts of their exposed skin, and they have significant scrapes on their arms and faces. Joe reaches to *his* face and rubs gently along a deep cut on his cheek. It is sore and still throbbing from being soaked in rainwater. The men should have more color than they do, and he wonders about his *own* color as he holds his scratched-up, pruned hands out in front of himself. His friends look more dead than alive within their state of deep sleep. He continues with his observations and scans the newest shack, looking for any evidence at all that may indicate someone other than them had been in there recently. He's discouraged by the notion that if there had been anybody else, any signs that may have been noticeable aren't anymore, as they had likely been destroyed last night when the men broke and entered, followed by Willy's subsequent outburst. Joe looks briefly at the pair of crammed-together single mattresses, then over to a dresser, and then down to a small, busted porcelain statue that lays in pieces by the far wall. At closer inspection, the statue seems to have been a samurai figurine. Unfortunately, there are no pieces big enough to re-purpose. Some of Willy's gutter spikes are also strewn about the floor.

He searches the dresser to find an old red-and-orange plaid shirt and a 1986 U.K. penny. The noise from Joe's rummaging wakes the men. He pockets the penny and drops the long-sleeved shirt on the top of the dresser.

"Cozy now," says Roe in his calm way of speaking. "Still raining a bit, I hear."

"Is that a dry shirt?" inquires Clive.

"Sure is," confirms Joe.

"Nice," says Clive, as he manages a full body stretch.

"Rock, paper, scissors ya for it!" says Willy excitedly.

"Let's do it," replies Clive, accepting the challenge.

"Now boys, Joe found it after all, he's entitled to first dibs," says Roe.

"No… You two go ahead," says Joe.

Willy puts his fist up from his bed.

Clive does the same from the floor. Willy counts to three and the two competitors pump their clenched fist in succession. "One, two, three." Willy shows scissors and cuts Clive's paper. As in any spirited bout of the age-old game, the loser of the first round sincerely sites the following as a rite of passage: "Best two out of three?" Clive is no exception and Willy ever equitable accepts the proposed extension thereby giving his opponent another chance. Clive's rock bashes Willy's scissors. The pair quickly move on to the third and deciding round where it is Willy's rocks turn to break Clive's scissors. "Vanquished!" exclaims the victor.

Roe gets to his feet and joins Joe at the dresser.

"Help me move this, will you, Boat?"

"That's my specialty," say Roebuck.

Roe tosses the shirt to Willy, and he and Joe move the dresser away from the door and back to its place.

"Got to tell that prick if we bump into him again that these are the worst accommodations ever," says Roebuck.

"Well, they *are* free," says Willy. Roe shoots him a look of disdain.

"I'm gonna go grab a drink," says Joe. He looks at Roebuck for a moment and walks outside. Roe calls out after him in a low voice, "I'll come with ya."

Clive and Willy look at each other nervously at the prospect of something going awry. They reach a nearby puddle and drink for a minute or two.

"Guess we got no choice but to press on, hey Joe?"

"Probably not, Boat."

"Can't just stick around in one of these sheds all day."

"Not after what happened to Charlie." Joe continues… "We can't seem to get that plan of traveling at night going."

Roe nods in agreement. "Y'know, as strange as all this is…and as much as I wish none of it had ever happened…and that it'd all just stop, I'm glad it's y'all that I have to go through it with… Being out here with you boys is…the only thing keepin' me sane," he confides.

Joe is silent for a moment, then places his hand on Roe's big shoulder. He feels that saying too much of anything back will understate the emotions he shares, so he chooses to simply say what is foremost on his mind and has been all the while. "We will make it."

"You crazy fuckers!" says Willy upon the pair arriving back inside the shack. He springs from the bed and onto his feet to change his shirt.

"Y'all didn't even make sure if it was safe."

"I had a feeling," says Joe.

Willy laughs. "A feeling, huh? I like that!" he says as he buttons his new, dry shirt up to the collar.

Before the men leave, they eat some cherries.

"Gettin' real low," says Willy. "They're almost gone."

Outside the shack, Clive and Willy drink their share from a deep puddle as Joe and Roebuck scan the forest. Clive fills his bottle for the road and plugs it. The men resume their pursuit of freedom after some debate about which way was *actually* north—what with running through the woods the night before in such an unorganized manner amidst the storm the group had lost track. Their conclusion is a slight muddied when they set out, but soon after observing the sun a while, they are all in agreement that the direction that they chose was indeed the correct one.

Later on, with the rain subsided and the sun glaring down from on high, the men are steadily making ground within the humidity and giving in to small talk.

"Pretty dry, considering," says Roe, of his pajamas. "Shoes are soggy though."

"I'm fucking starving," says Clive.

"I mean…he's quite the peacock, isn't he?" Willy says of their twisted stalker as he slings his slouching sack up further on his shoulder.

"He's completely insane. Speaking of which, we should keep it down, can't allow ourselves to get too comfortable out here," says Joe.

"Can we even be sure it's only *one* man out here?" proposes Clive.

"I think so," says Joe. "Charlie said the guy had a big, blond handlebar mustache. The bastard I saw had the same damn thing."

"Maybe it's required for the club membership," suggests Roe.

"Hey Willy," says Clive from beside him as they walk. "You wanna maybe…get rid of that bag? That meat *can't* be okay anymore."

"Clive, that bunny is long gone… Just the last bit of them cherries left in here now, and *those* are wrapped up nice and clean in a piece of cloth."

"Then why have the bag at all?"

"In case we need it for supplies man… Fuck!" shouts Willy as a branch sweeps alongside him, tearing a long scratch into his neck. Then, out of the clear blue sky, a shot rings out from behind them with a vicious bang. Willy is struck in the upper back. The bullet comes clean out of his chest. Clive is spattered with blood. Willy's arms flail upward and his fedora flies off as he falls forward to the ground.

"RUN!" shouts Clive. The three men instantly bolt fast through the woods. For an instant, Joe spins around to witness his badly injured friend struggle to his feet and clamber forward, where he is struck a second time in the back, Willy falls again and is still.

Joe scans the landscape. He can't place the shooter. He quickly turns to join the others dashing north and jumping and dodging obstacles. He meets up with Roe and Clive about one hundred yards away. They are catching their breath. Clive is angry as all the water from his bottle had spilled out during their sprint. He curses a blue streak.

Roe speaks urgently, "Did ya see him?"

"No," gasps Joe.

"Let's keep going, we're ahead of him now... Let's go!" Devoid of a sufficient break, the three men take off and continue to run north as fast as humanly possible. They halt after what seems like a mile.

Joe and Clive fall to their knees. Roe lands on all fours and vomits up what can only be cherry juice and rainwater.

They are covered in new cuts and bruises.

"Did you...see his hat fly off?" asks Clive, still out of breath, and for good reason. "It just...flew clean off." Roebuck lays fully out on his stomach as Joe, panting, gets to his feet. The men gradually collect their breath along with their composure.

When Roe finally rises, he is clearly wiping what is left of his tears.

"That boy," he says, "was my friend. He was manic, and he was unpredictable out here... He probably talked too much, but he was my friend... And I loved the son of a bitch." Roe wipes his last tear, "And I will miss him."

"He was a good man," agrees Joe. "He cared about you too...about all of us. Hell, he kept us from hunger. He found the matches that kept us warm."

"He was a good guy. I'll miss him too. We will *all* miss him," adds Clive.

Roe stares up to the sky and half-heartedly swats a fly away from his grubby face with a soiled hand. "What now, Joe?"

"That bastard is behind us… We got to go for it now… North as fast and as far as we can. To wherever it leads."

"And if it's nothing?" asks Roe

"What choice we got?" A moment passes. "It *will* be something," says Joe confidently. "I can feel it."

The three continue due north. They run and break and run and break. Repeating the same cycle, and doing the best they can to ignore their physical ailments and emotional stress. Finally, Clive gives in. "That shirt," he says. "Willy's Goddamn shirt," he adds while the men have briefly stopped and are recuperating.

"What of it?" asks Roe.

"I just can't help but wonder… if I had taken it, rather than accept his challenge and lose it to him, maybe it'd have been me laying back there."

"That's crazy talk," says Roe. "Why would you think that?"

"Because maybe…it was the best target…for that madman…the bright red and orange colors, I mean."

"It's wonders like that that drive a man crazy. You don't give that kind of thinkin' another second!" says Roe.

"Clive!" says Joe, firmly. "*I* found that shirt and very well could have put it on *myself*, and it is me who presented it to you all. It's nothing… It was just a shirt! Okay, Clive? Besides…it's *his* fault we're out here…dyin'! That we're being hunted like animals. This is about *more* than a red-and-orange shirt."

Clive feels ashamed to have allowed the bigger picture to elude him. "Yeah... Okay Joe, you're right," agrees Clive. "Can we assume that guy has had his fill for today?" he asks.

"Seems we can't assume a whole lot out here," interjects Roe.

"If we don't escape this forest, I don't know how we'll beat him. How we'll ever survive. Feels like it's inevitable... Our demise... He took us as if we were his own personal fucked-up playthings to be toyed with. He's killed four that we know of. It feels like our days here are numbered."

"That's enough Clive!" cries Joe. "You can't say that. Don't say that, we *must* remain positive!"

"...and then what's he do with the dead?" continues Clive, disregarding Joe's plea.

"Does he fuckin' eat the bodies? Maybe he displays the heads."

"Clive!" shouts Joe. "Get it together! We must *believe* we are going to figure it out, going to make it...going to survive!" Joe walks over, grabs Clive by the shoulders, and looks him in the eyes. "Do not panic, we are going to get free...we must...right?"

"Right Joe, you're right."

"We're with you Joe," says Roebuck with a nod. He releases Clive. Roe pats his friend on the shoulder. "We'll pull it together." he says with a deeply determined expression. The three ran until they were numb and continue through the forest silently. They are exhausted as they meticulously weave through the woods, making decent progress.

"We'll just keep on going till we can't walk no more," announces Roe.

There is no protest from the others. They are weak, hungry, thirsty, and in dire need of a long rest.

The afternoon sun shines warm and bright as innocent sounds flow through the wilds.

"I'm dry," says Clive with a surprisingly relieved tone of voice. It's the first time he has spoken in hours. "Bone-dry," he adds, forcing a smile.

"Yeah, me too… Feels amazing," says Joe.

Roe shakes his pajama top. We're dry because it's damn hot. "Time for a drink," he says as he points out a small pond. Joe, Clive, and Roebuck stagger to it. They kneel down beside the murky, standing water and drink from cupped hands until satiated. They sit awhile afterwards, too spent to move. Their physical energy low as well as their mental acuity. Joe looks to the treetops. He watches a pair of blue jays fly effortlessly, way above.

"Man, those guys got it easy, eh?" he says as he slowly nudges Clive for his attention. He nods up toward them.

"I'll say," agrees Clive from his daze, as he too looks to the birds in the sky.

Roe glances up from his reflection as well. "If only we could fly away, hey boys?"

"Those birds…we have *got* to be north," says Joe.

"Well we are, we've been heading that way all day," says Roebuck.

"No…I mean north…the north country…somewhere."

Clive looks back down at his skewed reflection in the water's choppy surface. He doesn't recognize what he sees. He recites Poe, one of his favorite classic authors to himself, under his breath. "All that we see or seem is but a dream within a dream."

"What's that?" asks Joe. Clive is in a trance…

"Maybe we are all a dream and we are in one together."

# 21
# What If?

It is sunny and hot. Weak and weary, the men travel onward. Laboriously navigating the seemingly endless, harrowing wilderness. They are filthy, their clothes are tattered, and their bodies are beaten.

*Are these guys ever lookin' frail,* thinks Roebuck as he studies his friends.

Willy's infamous rabbit meat and overripe cherries had only held them for so long.

"I always wanted to lose a few pounds, but not this way," says Roebuck with forced cheer, trying to lighten the mood.

"What if this place is hell?" inquires Clive, of his own suggestion.

"What if we're already dead, and the devil himself is our merciless stalker in an infinite, torturous playground of his own design?"

Rather than dismantle Clive's notion aloud, both men remain silent and in their collective haze, they regretfully consider it a viable possibility.

They trudge forth on sore, battered feet. The trio drinks from puddles and avoid the numerous added obstructions the storm left behind within their invisible, northern pathway. After a lengthy stretch without a break, the men cross a glen.

Joe and Clive find themselves crouched down at another watering hole.

Joe looks above after splashing his face and saturating his hair. Their stops to rehydrate almost always instantly invigorate the men, however temporary it may be. He inspects some downed branches entangled within a massive oak tree. "That tree is enormous," he says as he stands up. "Keep your eyes peeled guys for tall trees that we might be able to climb. If we can get to the top of the tree-line, maybe we'll be able to see…something, *anything*."

Roebuck is nearby, at the base of a large maple, rooting through some broken branches within a small cluster. He chooses for himself, a long, thick, relatively straight branch with two points. He uses it as a walking stick and approaches the other two men. "Not bad pickins'," he says as he motions back toward the tree trunk. The three carry on.

"What'll you do if you make it outta here?" asks Clive as they walk closely together.

"You mean, *when* we get out of here," says Joe.

Clive manages a half smile.

"There's a woman…who I'd taken for granted. I will reach out to her," answers Joe. "What about you Clive?"

"Eat, sleep… Not sure in what order," he adds.

Roebuck remains silent as he walks along, in front of them.

"What about you Rowboat?" asks Clive.

A quiet moment passes. "Visit my dad," he replies.

Later, the men are indulging in a much-needed rest. Clive is laid out on a spot within some long grass and leaned back against a large tree trunk. He impulsively pulls some of the grass out of the ground and begins to eat it, unenthusiastically. Joe is sitting atop a boulder covered in moss, and Roe is seated cross-legged by a large Sumac bush.

"Well, I suppose I'll need a new work shirt," says Clive, looking down at his ragged clothing. He examines them a moment and looks back up in the direction of his friends. "That there…it looks edible…the red parts," he says of the bush behind Roe.

"I'm not sure of any damn plant in these here woods."

"The juniper…that I found Charlie under…can't get that one out of my mind. That's a northern bush, is it not?" quizzes Joe. There is no response from the other downtrodden men. "Those red buds there, or whatever they are, could be okay…but then again who the hell knows."

"Fuck," exclaims Clive.

"Yeah," says Joe in agreement to his friend's well asserted expletive. "Do you guys recall the story of Chris McCandless?" he adds. Roe shakes his head in sorrow, "Jesus Christ," he whispers, regarding the reference just cited. The men sit in silence a moment.

"Well… I gotta see a man about a mule," says Roebuck. A euphemism intended to lighten the mood. He stands up using his walking stick for leverage.

Clive closes his eyes and leans his head back on the tree behind him. "I'd eat a mule steak."

Roe walks slowly through the foliage and disappears out of sight into the bushes. Upon relieving himself, he hears a rustle to his left and steps quietly toward the sound.

He observes the bushes before him as they shake and vibrate. The commotion stops for a moment and then continues again. Suddenly, a large, brown-feathered partridge flaps its wings as it presents itself. It motions to skitter right past Roebuck. He instinctively and without hesitation swings down fast and clubs the bird as hard as he can, connecting perfectly with its head. He bludgeons the partridge two more times where it lays to end its suffering and lay his claim on the animal. Joe is standing there when Roebuck spins around after picking up the bird with his free hand.

Clive appears shocked when Roebuck and Joe come out of the brush with the partridge hanging upside down, its body limp and its large wings spread out. Roebuck has it clutched by the ankles in his large fist.

"Oh my God!" exclaims Clive as he gets to his feet.

"Not quite a mule, but not too bad either," says Roe.

"Wouldn't Willy a' just went crazy over this?" he adds as he sets the bird on a nearby boulder. The men stand surrounding the partridge for a few moments. The blood drains slowly from its small head to a pool on the large rock before welling over and streaming alongside it and dripping off into the grass. "Now I'd hunted for fowl many a time in my younger days with my daddy, and it's difficult, even with a hound and rifle. This is something else… This is a gift," says Roe.

Clive looks the bird all over. "Raw poultry. Will we be sick?" he asks.

"We're already sick."

"Let's risk it then. Let's get at it and just put some of this into our stomachs fast, but I can't tear away at that animal," says Clive.

"I'll do it," affirms Roebuck.

"Here, this may help," says Joe, handing him his makeshift dagger. Clive turns away quickly as Roe proceeds to pull the feathers from the partridge's breast. Joe turns around too a few times and winces. It is a purely savage sight. Roebuck plunges the steel into the deceased animal and its leg begins to twitch.

He shreds long, slimy pieces of meat from its body. Exorbitant amount of blood pours out all over the rock as he defiles the animal, setting strips and chunks all over the boulder in piles. He stacks flesh on one side and useless parts on the other.

"I'm gonna let it bleed out a couple minutes," he says as he wipes his red hands on his pajama bottoms. There is blood all over his front side.

After a minute or two, he scavenges some more meat from the body of the bird, until the collection is ample. He picks up a decent portion from the cache. Clive finally faces the partridge's heavily mutilated carcass. He dry-heaves at the unrecognizable sight. "We'll all have some, huh?" asks Clive as he mentally prepares for what he is about to do.

"I... I don't know," says Joe.

"Willy seemed to get along with that old rabbit meat. I gotta take my chances here fellas," says Roebuck as he kneels down and runs a large strip through a nearby shallow puddle. His friends watch as he doesn't hesitate to put it into his mouth. He bites down. The strip of flesh is very slimy and especially chewy.

"Lord," says Roe with watered down blood on his lips and chin. "It's wrong, it's just so wrong!" he says assertively.

"Oh, man," says Roe as Clive again begins to dry-heave and spit up puddle water, bits of grass, and stomach bile.

Roebuck swallows and hunches over. He puts his hands on the ground and waits a moment.

"It feels good in the old belly for now, though," he laughs. "Feeling energized already," he adds. "Goddamn, I really am...and hell! Maybe that prick'll get me before I come up too sick, eh boys?"

"Fuck!" exclaims Clive. He pushes himself to snatch a chunk of the wild poultry. "I'm not going to let you die of some type of fucked up food poisoning without me!" he says excitedly before gobbling down the portion. With Joe looking on, the two men reluctantly eat a couple more pieces of meat; and with their faces and hands as red as can be, they stuff their pockets with meat.

"What are we becoming?" asks Clive as he looks at his hands.

"We're desperate, is all," replies Roe sternly. "We've held out long enough…as long as we could."

"We need to eat.… We're trying to survive…right Joe?"

The men are silent as they hang on for Joe's answer. As if what they hear might make them feel more civilized.

"Yeah boys… We're surviving," he says finally.

With renewed stamina, the pair clean up as thoroughly as they can at a nearby puddle. They scrub and rinse their hands and faces rigorously.

The men utilize the rest of the day to the fullest and walk with great persistence.

As the sun sets, the fatigued travelers agree to stop for sleep. They had put in a good day of progress and cannot muster any more exertion and so make their bed in a clearing within the cool, long green grass. They are hidden well, and the woods surround them with distant, tall trees. The stars come out in bunches. The men stare longingly into space and at the moon as they lay side by side, on their backs. Roebuck and Clive are relieved that the partridge meat had not yet made them sick. The men trade basic knowledge of the constellations and try to identify some of them.

"In world so beautiful, it's sad all the ugliness that transpires within it at times," says Clive from his place between Roebuck and Joe.

"Amen to *that*," agrees Roe.

"It's so awful, what happened to the others… I can't get Willy outta my head," says Clive.

A moment passes.

"Who's taking first watch?" asks Joe.

"Another night off would be just the thing," says Roebuck.

The men lay quietly, listening to the peaceful, natural sounds within the forest.

"Amen to that," agrees Joe.

It seems like every star is present, scattered, and shining brightly as they shimmer in intervals.

One shoots across the sky magnificently as the men fall asleep.

# 22

# A Long Time

It is still and quiet. A patch of Alumroot absorbs the strong rays of morning sunshine. The light accentuates their vivid shades of green.

The shrubs begin to shake imperceptibly at first, then more obviously. Out steps the hunter; the phantom stalker who so cold-heartedly aspires to kill his fellow man.

He is adorned, head to toe, in an American Civil war era confederate general's uniform. Not one piece of gray is missing. He grips the out of place German Jäger rifle he so adores. Its gold plates gleam. As he creeps the forest, he does so with an arrogant composure. He is pensive and almost robotically crosses a clearing opposite the Alumroot and does so carefully before vanishing into a cluster of spruce trees.

"How do we wake up from the nightmare?" asks Clive as they walk.

"We survive it… We see it through to the end," answers Joe as he notices a red maple tree to his right. He sees something that strikes his interest and goes to it. The men surround it and get close too. He examines the tree trunk and points out a chiseled inscription. He puts his partridge blood encrusted dagger in his hand and reaches out. Mimicking the letter *J*, he follows along with the tip of the tarnished steels rusty blade. He moves across the *O* and then finishes off at the final letter, the *E*. The inscription is thick and legible but also faded in gray, and it appears to have been done a long time ago.

"We gotta be getting close," says Clive as they examine the etches. Upon further inspection, they discover a thinner, less-obvious carving underneath. "1886," says Roebuck, squinting at it.

"That's a 9," imparts Joe.

"Yeah, 1986…maybe that maniac's name," suggests Clive.

"Maybe a victim," mumbles Joe.

"Maybe neither," interjects Roe. "Let's keep on going," he adds.

Clive follows Roe away from the maple. Joe continues his analysis for a moment more before catching up.

"Don't let it spook ya, Joe," says Roebuck.

Throughout the day, Clive begins to turn somewhat ill. He is especially nauseated and weak. The men may have considered blaming it solely on the raw meat from the day before, but Roe feels fine in that regard.

Clive does his best, however, to keep up with his friends and not let on too much about how he truly feels. As they venture forth, Roebuck stops and displays a rare out-pouring of emotion.

"How have we *not* gotten to a *road*!" he cries. "This is insane!" The big man tries to control himself, but he succumbs to his pent-up feelings and lets out a thunderous, steady, prolonged yell. Any birds within earshot leave the area. Joe and Clive stand together as they observe their friend.

"Fuck this place," says Clive, under his breathe.

"It really *is* unbelievable… *Nothing* for days and days," agrees Joe. "Just think though, how beautiful it will be when freedom finally presents itself… And it will happen *fast*… It will be right there."

As another agonizing day comes and goes, dusk settles down onto the forest in magnificent arrays of orange and pink. The men stop at a stretch of shallow creek, where they take a break to drink. "Too tired and hungry to hike through hell tonight," states Roe as he splashes his face. "Y'know, the water here in the woods is one of the best things we got going." He pulls a cut of partridge meat from his shirt's front pocket, rinses it, and puts it in his mouth.

Joe watches Roe a moment and then Clive "How do you feel Clive?"

He looks over to Joe from his squat at the edge of the creek. He is white, his lips are chapped, and his eyes are dark and sunken. "This is never going to end. I have it figured… This *is* our hell."

The men walk a little further.

They discover a large boulder in the distance, surrounded by thorn bushes and underneath a giant ash tree. They carefully maneuver themselves between the bushes. Clive and Roebuck sit leaning with their backs against the enormous rock.

"How long do you think we've been here?" asks Clive.

"Way too long. We don't even know how long we were gone before we were dumped in those sheds or how long we were there," says Roe.

"I don't know," says Clive. "I just don't know… Feels like eternity," he says as he looks up at the darkening sky.

"What do you think Joe?" asks Roebuck. Joe is still standing, looking into the deep, green oblivion. He presses the tip of his steel dagger with his thumb. "A long time," he says.

"I don't know what's gonna get me first, a bullet, this sickness, or starvation," says Clive. Irritated, he aggressively takes his share of partridge meat from his pockets and tosses it off into the thorns and then in aggravation firmly wipes the palms of his hands on his pants.

"I got first watch," announces Joe as he stares ahead into the dark woods. Soon, the moon takes control of the night's sky.

It is a warm, bright summer day outside of Joe's workshop. The double-doors on its front-side slowly open to reveal Joe standing over a freshly built birdhouse. A young woman slowly walks in with her long, dark hair flowing, shiny and smooth down her back. She exudes an extraordinary radiance and classic, natural beauty.

"You're home!" he calls out as he turns from his work to embrace her.

"I'll never leave you again," he says.

"You promise?" whispers the woman. Joe wakes up with a gasp to a morning as bright as can be.

"You okay?" asks Roe from his spot on the grass nearby.

Joe squints and looks all around as the thorn bushes come into focus from below.

"Yeah, I'm okay." He rises to his feet and looks outward from their hiding place.

A moment passes, while he observes the forest until he is briefly pulled back into his fantasy. He imagines the woman disappear and the doors of his workshop slam shut, with immense force. They are left to shudder. "Let's get on with this," says Joe.

It takes great effort, but they finally wake Clive and start out.

"These days are all bleeding into each other. It feels awful that we've lost track," confides Joe.

"Fuck," mutters Roebuck.

Shortly thereafter, the men rehydrate themselves at the nearby creek once again.

Clive, who has yet to speak after the night before, stays sat down by it, longer than the others. His face is blank and there is a vacancy behind his eyes. He notices a small grub evade his presence and wriggle underneath a rock and into the damp earth. He slowly turns his head and glares down a moment, to the ground, then rolls the rock over and easily uncovers the grub and stares some more before coming to life and digging deeper into the dirt with his fingers. He excavates a few loose handfuls of soil to reveal a half dozen or so more. "I don't know boys," he whispers softly. Clive clears his throat and speaks up, impulsively. "I… I have to," he declares loudly. "If I do, will you?" he asks. The men don't answer. They are stood off away from the creek and can't make exact sense of what he is saying. They come closer. He takes a handful of grubs from their dwelling and watches them as they wiggle around and squirm on the palm of his hand. He quickly gobbles them down, dirt and all.

Clive gags and coughs violently. Seemingly against his will, he clambers to pick up a few more and maniacally eats them too.

"Fuck!" he shouts, as a strand of thick drool hangs from his bottom lip. "Boat, there's still more!"

"The meat I got it's…it's doing me just fine for now," says Roe. Clive quickly leans forward and dunks his head into the water. He struggles to take in and drink as much as he can manage, then sits back up and buries his drenched face into his soiled hands. He slowly fights to catch his breath within the thin layer of mud. Joe and Roebuck watch patiently as they wait for their friend. When ready, the men continue advancing through the wilderness.

A few miles through the forest, they are absolutely stunned when a massive, abandoned, two-story barn reveals itself through the trees. For the worn-out travelers, the enormous building is an unexpected, eerie sight. First its buckled, partially caved in, rusted roof comes into view, then its sagging exterior; slouched wooden walls covered in vines, and finally a few of its open, crooked doorways present themselves. Varying large bushes have been slowly but surely reclaiming the structure through the years. The dilapidated building's roof has darkened to a deep brown and its walls have faded to a washed-out tone of gray.

Once the men get over the initial shock and the subsequent reality of their discovery sinks in, they can hardly subdue their excitement for what the presence of the barn could mean and what useful things they might find there inside. As much as they want to explore it right away, they know all too well that they must beware, incase their pursuer is in the vicinity or worse still, has set a trap. The trio wait quietly for a while amongst the brush, before approaching.

A half an hour passes of excruciating anticipation until the men head directly to the relic through a small clearing. Slow at first, then gradually to a jog. They stop beside the long side of the building closest to their previous position. Joe looks inside through a knothole before making his way along the wall a short distance toward the front of the barn and through the nearest open doorway. Roe and Clive follow just behind. "Unbelievable!" says Roebuck. "It's a goddamn haven!"

The barn's main floor is wide-open and empty. It is obvious that most of the interior had been stripped away and removed ages ago. Along the sides there are a few dusty benches and some warped cabinets. At the back, opposite the men, there are eight gated box stalls built into the structure and in front of them is a rickety wooden ladder, leading up to the partial floor of a loft area. The floor is doubling as the stalls ceiling. There are mounds of loose straw in the loft and stacks of abandoned square hay bales throughout.

"We've got to be getting close now," says Joe as he scans the building. Upon spotting the loft, Clive climbs the ladder and allows himself to fall backwards into the straw. Roe searches the first floor for anything of value.

The men's confidence is restored every second they are inside the barn.

Joe joins Roebuck within the search while Clive lay still on the straw, surely the most comfortable he'd been in a while. Among the countertops. There is nothing of much use; just a few empty containers and canisters of old, unrecognizable products. Most of the labels are not legible. Joe analyzes a small, semi-transparent, capped, one hundred milliliter plastic container. It is the cleanest bottle among them that can easily fit in his back pocket, so he tightens the lid and slides it inside his jeans. They eagerly open all the drawers and cupboards within the cabinetry only to find filth and grime. Soon, the pair makes their way across the barn and they search each stall one by one. All eight are completely empty. Suddenly, Clive calls out from the loft, "Fellas, up here! Quick! Come quick!" The men race up the ladder to join Clive.

They arrive at the loft to see a cat coming toward him.

"Shhh," he whispers. Clive is on his knees, with a hand reaching out in front of him. "Here kitty, kitty."

The cat is a bold, bright white female with deep blue eyes. As she crawls over, she begins to purr and when she arrives at Clive's side, she rolls in the straw. The feline seems healthy and her coat appears clean. The cat is wearing a red collar around her neck with a shiny, gold circular pendant dangling from it. He gently pets their visitor and takes her into his arms. He carefully grabs the medallion with his fingers and reads the engraving aloud, "HOPE."

Clive lets her go. She jumps back into the straw. Wide-eyed, he turns to look up at his friends and covers his mouth briefly with his hand. He rises to his feet.

"Her neck! She has a collar! Her name is Hope!" exclaims Clive.

"She's a house cat." says Roe. Clive can barely contain himself. "Where do we go? Which way? Which way boys? We gotta go!" He urges the others to offer up quick council.

Roe closes his eyes and bows his head in relief, as if their nightmare had ended right then and there.

"Wait!" says Joe, firmly. "Just wait… We must remain cautious," he says as he wrestles with his own reeling emotions.

"Let's watch her," says Clive. "She'll show us the way; maybe it's not far, it could be right out there!"

He turns to look for her, but she is gone. "Hey! SHIT! We could have followed her. What the hell!" He runs to a wide gap between two boards at the back wall of the barn and glares outside to the ground.

"Damn it!" shouts Clive. "She could have helped us!"

"She already did," says Joe.

# 23

# Hope

Despite Clive's persistent protest, the men wait a little while in the barn. They contemplate the possibility of climbing onto the roof for a better look at the landscape surrounding them and search one last time for anything worth taking. Roebuck finds a dull, half-inch-wide hand chisel with a rotten wooden handle underneath a bench. With nowhere practical enough to hold it within his pajamas, he forces the tool into the only available place, the front pocket of his shirt. He puts it in blade down and intentionally pierces a slot in through the bottom of it, revealing the rusty protrusion below and outside the front of the shirt and leaving the handle snug on the inside of the pocket. Clive quickly gives up his half-hearted investigation and returns to the place on the straw atop the loft. Joe's latest search comes up empty. Before long, the men are sitting together amongst the mounds of straw. The sense of ambition that they feel is elevated to new heights and it is obvious in their collective demeanor. Clive is particularly motivated and, most of all, excited. Any signs of doubt are replaced by a confidence that is unparalleled to that of his behavior in the days leading up to their encounter with Hope.

The men finally agree to leave the barn but sit in silence for a moment. Each mentally prepares in their own way to continue their journey through the forest.

"All I know is that when we get free…we all ought to stay connected…y'all are my friends," says Roebuck. "I expect to hear from you guys from time to time," he adds.

"I wouldn't have it any other way, Rowboat," confirms Joe.

"Absolutely," agrees Clive.

"Good, now let's get the fuck outta here." The men collect themselves and exit the barn with their newfound energy. They case the building to decide whether or not it is worth finding a way up on to the roof. After careful consideration, they surmise that it is not tall enough or stable enough to risk the time and effort it would take to get on top of it. The men hike north for about a half an hour before their frustration begins to resurface,

"Where's the road? Where's the fucking houses? Which direction should we go?" cries Clive.

Another stressful half an hour goes by. They advance through trees and bushes and down an incline, to where they notice something out of sorts propped up and leaning on the far side of a large rock about ten yards ahead of them, in a thinner patch of the woods. They motion to each other to stay quiet and approach the object. They stop within some bushes near the tree line of the clearing's perimeter.

"Wait… Let's be sure," suggests Joe. They wait a moment.

"I'll go check it out," whispers Roebuck. He leaves Joe and Clive, staying low as he heads toward the object. He arrives at the rock to find that what is leaning up against its opposite side is the infamous gold-plated West German C.E.T.M.E. assault Jäger rifle with a Nazi issued S.S. captain's hat set on the tip of its barrel. Wide-eyed, Roe drops his walking stick and analyzes the silver eagle adorned on the front of the hat and the silver skull below it. He quickly knocks the hat off and picks up the rifle as if he's just discovered the Holy Grail. He studies it briefly with an overwhelming fascination.

Joe and Clive look on in anticipation of Roe's findings.

"What does he have?" asks Clive. Roebuck raises the rifle to the air with one hand to show his friends. Stunned as the rifle's profile becomes clear, the men jog to meet Roe. They study the weapon a few seconds before simultaneously looking all around for the gun's owner. Roe cocks the rifle.

All is silent as they scan the woods.

Suddenly, Joe shouts, in terror, "It's a set-up!"

The man with the mustache charges out of the trees from the east and in front of them. He is outfitted in an M-1940 Nazi field general's army uniform. The tunic, complete with rank defining insignias cut past his waist, has a decorated high collar and shoulder-straps and four, large, pleated, round-edged pockets along its front-side. He wears matching M-40 field trousers, tucked into black jackboots. They appear to have been recently polished. He raises his left hand and points a rare Parisian long-barrel Luger pistol, model 1314, right toward Roe.

Roebuck raises the rifle toward their nemesis and pulls the trigger…the chamber is empty. The killer unloads three bullets in quick succession into Roe's chest as he marches forward. Roebuck falls backwards and as he does, the butt of the rifle hits the ground. The shooter snatches the gun with his free hand before it falls over on his way by Roe. He proceeds to follow Joe and Clive, who are scrambling northward, and fires two shots in their direction. They find their footing and disappear into the trees. The man turns back toward Roe and, without more than a glance or break in stride, shoots a bullet into Roe's forehead as he walks back by to collect his hat. He picks it up, dusts it off, and puts it on his head. Roebuck lays dead behind his killer in a puddle of pooling blood, his blue pajamas almost completely red. In an instant, he too turns and vanishes northbound.

"He must have been watching us all the time!" shouts Clive while catching his breath.

"We don't know that for certain. C'mon, we gotta continue pushing north—" says Joe, loudly.

"He's toying with us! God damn it!" interrupts Clive.

"It's just the two of us now Clive! Just you and I…okay?"

"I can't believe it! I thought we were saved, that it'd be over soon!" cries Clive.

"It will be! It will be! We are getting close."

"What now? Joe, what now?"

"We go forward. North! He's behind us again! No time to waste. Let's move!"

The men take off further north. Soon, the run regresses to a hike. Their energy has plummeted. They keep silent until they stop beneath a giant elm.

"He might be hunting us by night now," says Joe.

"What do you mean?" asks Clive urgently.

"I mean, we can't stop too much anymore. He looked angry and I don't think those were warning shots this time… He wants to end this. I can feel it."

The two men leave the elm behind and walk till dusk.

"I need to stop," announces Clive. "I can't go anymore, my whole body is numb."

"Mine too."

They take cover amongst a heavily wooded area and set themselves down. "We'll get there real soon," proclaims Joe as he examines his dagger beneath the setting sun.

"I feel like I'm already dead… I can't take much more, I'm losing it," says Clive firmly.

"Sleep. I've got watch." Clive closes his eyes.

Joe looks to the orange and blue layers in the sky through the trees. Though Roebuck's death was just as tragic, it somehow didn't resonate the same way with him as the other murders did. In a strange way, a friend dying had become expected, and since Willy's demise, Joe had begun to feel hardened and devoid of much emotion. With Roe's death the reality also came that the end is near, that the story in the forest is almost over.

The moon shines full. All is at peace when Joe wakes up in the middle of the night. He looks into the starry sky from his back; he feels as if his friends are watching down on him and Clive.

He feels unexpectedly secure and empowered. A responsibility of sorts. He looks over at Clive as he sleeps, then back up to the stars, and closes his eyes too.

He remembers Charlie and how much he learned from him about their perilous conundrum. He remembers Willy, his unorthodox humor and generous ways. Then, he thinks of Roebuck and the composure he had and his thoughtful leadership qualities.

Joe tries to imagine Simon and Neil… The men he did not meet. He wonders how *he'd* be remembered. He tells himself to have courage and, despite fear, believes that they will all soon be free, one way or another.

Joe recalls a quote his mother has on a bronzed scroll hanging on her dining room wall: 'Faith is the substance of things hoped for, the evidence of things not seen.'

## 24
# Death from Above

A biplane from aviation's 'pioneer era' rips through the clear blue sky. It's a Weaver aircraft. The two-seater flies low to the forest but still way above Joe and Clive as it tilts and turns with its stacked wings. It is scouting the woods.

Joe and Clive are abruptly awoken to the sound of the tail dragging and the two-stoker engine sweeping southbound.

"Stay low!" shouts Joe as it sails by.

"What the hell!" calls Clive. "What if it's help?"

Joe examines the machine. It's got a tan body with red wings. He is momentarily stunned as he sees the large capital letters; J.O.E, painted underneath them in bold, black font. He recalls his little lakeside cottage in Southeastern Ontario, and how, now and then, two-seater biplanes would fly gingerly above as he watched, beer in hand, from a lawn chair on his front deck. Those planes fitted with the sky. *This* looks like something the Wright brothers would have flown.

Clive looks to Joe in anticipation.

"It's him!" he cries. The aircraft tilts its body and circles back. It cruises slowly as it coasts northbound, back south, and north again. The relentless hunter is quite obviously and methodically surveying the wild. They clamber below a tree, so as to stay well-hidden. "We need to pay attention! And listen once it's outta sight, to hear which direction he goes when he leaves!" shouts Joe. Clive nods.

After a few minutes and several slow laps above the forest, the plane finishes its last sweep of the area and passes them by.

"Listen to it," says Clive.

The aircraft heads north. The men stay still, concentrating, on the sound of the plane as it gradually fades, not to return.

"North!" shouts Joe. "It's the right way!"

"YES!" exclaims Clive with a smile not seen since back at the barn. "Whatever's up ahead," he adds, "We gotta be ready."

The men hike fast through the wilderness, confident that, at least for a while, there will be no danger.

An hour passes, and the pair begin to slow down. Their adrenaline has waned, and they are back to applying the careful tactics that they've adopted so well. They know enough time has passed that the hunter could be on foot and tracking them again and if he is, there's a chance he'll be in front of them.

They stop at a small pond and drink.

"It kinda feels like *we're* chasing after *him*...he's left us his trail anyway...and it feels good." Clive ponders a moment and continues... "Whatever's up there, it has *got* to be civilization, hasn't it?"

"It has to be," says Joe whole-heartedly.

They look at each other, fully aware that it is down to them. They've lost so much to this point and now must carry the torch for themselves and the fallen. Whether it was the cat, the plane, or both. The men share a common strength between them.

"No grubs?" asks Joe, as he fills and caps his bottle.

"Not today," replies Clive.

"I was stoked up to give 'em a try."

"Bullshit!"

Joe laughs, playfully.

"Y'know what would be alright?" remarks Clive.

"Probably a whole lot of things," Joe laughs again.

"One of Willy's Lucky Strikes."

"Yeah," agrees Joe as he looks down at his reflection and pinches all along his beard, under his chin. He barely recognizes himself. Clive slowly fills his glass bottle full and then holds it just under the surface of the water. He releases it and watches as it sinks and fades away.

The men continue their hike into the calm of the afternoon, when finally, they halt, as an unusual series of noises sound off ahead of them amidst the nearby northern part of the woods, prompting them to immediately get low and take cover behind a large rock. They focus on the disturbance.

"Should we run?" whispers Clive, as the sounds in the woods draw closer.

"No, not yet." Joe closes his eyes, takes out his dagger and grips it tight, as to try to channel away some of the stress. There is something there, not far from them. Moving. He imagines the doe from his shack and the hollow. With all his might, he visualizes her coming out of the woods in front of them. Just then, a shot rings out and ricochets off the top of the rock, snapping Joe from his daydream.

A bit of stone dust billows upward and hangs in the air, as Clive darts out from their spot and runs quickly northeast into the nearby thicket. Joe imagines himself getting hemmed in and shot in the head, and that's enough for him to get going too. He inhales deep and dashes toward the forest where Clive disappeared. As he enters the trees, another shot rings out, taking a chunk out of a long needle pine tree to Joe's left. He runs as fast as he can.

After running through, jumping over, and dodging around countless obstacles within the unforgiving terrain, he meets up with Clive. They slow to a stop.

Unable to advance without a break, Clive falls to the ground. Joe falls too. The two lay on their backs, staring at the sky through the trees. "He missed us," says Clive. "Missed us both, for the first time, he *missed* us," he repeats. "We're ahead of him again," says Joe. "We should go!"

They stumble to their feet. Two more gunshots rip through the woods, sending the pair fleeing forward even faster, they duck behind a cluster of dense bushes and stay still.

"Fuck, fuck, fuck," whispers Joe, as he searches his mind for a plan. "Clive, what do you think about splitting up this duo for a while?"

"For a *while*?" repeats Clive.

"Yes, it could double our chances of success. We both know we're headed generally north, no matter what. You head north by northeast, I'll head north by northwest and whoever reaches safety first, sends for help. Send every local cop, state trooper, A.T.F., F.B.I., everyone that can be found out here and anyone else who can be contacted. The entire fuckin' cavalry!" exclaims Joe. "What do you think?"

"We're close. We are *definitely* close," he adds.

"Mmhm," agrees Clive as he nods his head slowly up and down. He thinks for a moment "Okay, okay. Let's go for it!" Clive looks Joe directly in the eyes and puts out his hand. The men shake.

"We will go with the spirit of all the men lost here," proclaims Joe.

Clive smiles. "See you on the other side." And with that, he turns and quickly goes north and slightly east. Joe goes north and slightly west. As he does, he recalls a part of a simple, yet powerful scripture he learned when he was a boy. Joe whispers it to himself, "Be strong and of good courage. Do not fear or be afraid."

A half an hour passes. He thinks about the friends he's met in the forest and his forgotten life as he hikes forth, doing his best to keep alert and on the defensive. Joe thinks about Clive and imagines him sprinting across an open field to a small town on the other side. Suddenly, his positive thoughts dispel. He is jolted back to reality when a bang in the distance to his right sounds off and echoes through the forest to the east. A faint, disturbing scream of agony follows the harsh reverberation. Clive's cry seems to flow through the area like an unrelenting, wave. It instantly courses through the woods.

Joe is haunted. He knows what's coming next. All he can do is wait…

After a moment, the sound of another shot bellows through the forest. Joe's heart sinks. He lowers his head, closes his eyes, and his legs begin to shake. He stumbles a few feet forward. Though he fights it, he is brought down to one knee.

"No," he whispers. He buries his face in his hands. Joe is alone.

# 25

# Alone

The last man runs through the woods with the weight of the world on his shoulders. If he is caught and killed, who will ever tell their story? He traverses the rugged terrain. Who will be the one to hold this evil man accountable? *If not myself, then no man perhaps,* he thinks. He feels like the only person on the planet and as if the six other men's souls reside with him at the very same time. Joe is inspired by the reality that to obtain even a glimpse of closure, he *must* survive. As his worries dissipate, an intense anger begins to brew. A will grows more powerful than any he had before during his time in the forest and it is bound with an utmost responsibility. It is up to him alone and he intends to give everything he can to make it through. Minutes turn into hours, and hours into dusk. Joe walks as the sun sets and disappears. He walks in the hope that manmade light will reveal itself in the dark. Joe can no longer see very far in front of him and blocks out the eerie sounds of animals as they carry on around him. He maintains his composure as he walks. Searching for perfect cover is less important now, as he is just one. When he feels he must rest, he enters a heavily wooded area and gets as comfortable as possible on his back, beneath a large pine tree. The area underneath is clear and flat. At first, Joe tries to sleep with one eye open and an ear to the ground, but he doesn't. He's counting on a big day tomorrow, so he gives in and closes his eyes. *The first day of the rest of my life*, he thinks to himself, before entering the peculiar state between reality and dream. He is ten years old and back in his childhood church with his grandmother. He looks up to her face from his seat beside her on the heavily glazed, solid-oak pew and then past the starched suits and dresses of the adults in front of him and toward the sermon. The group is prompted to rise. He can smell strong blends of the people's colognes and perfumes as he stands there amongst them, surrounded.

He looks between the crowd and on ahead to see an elderly man standing on stage, front and center, behind a pulpit. The man begins to talk in a monotone with his arms extended and held out beside himself and his palms facing forward.

Little Joseph, as his doting grandmother would often call him, whispers meekly along with the boisterous congregation…

*"Saint Michael the Archangel, defend us in battle.*

*Be our protection against the wickedness and snares of the devil;*

*May God rebuke him, we humbly pray; and do thou, O prince of the Heavenly Host, by the power of God, thrust into hell Satan and all evil spirts, who wander through the world, for the ruin of souls. Amen."*

…Joe is asleep.

As the sun rises it brings with it an especially warm and bright, beautiful morning. A blue jay is perched on the treetop of the pine tree. Underneath, a baby rabbit hops gingerly to his side. The animal sniffs his hand for a moment and slowly bounds off as a goldfinch skitters by.

Joe's fingers retract, as he slowly wakes up. He swipes at the ground where the rabbit had been with a delayed reaction. Upon coming to, he looks up through the pine and out to the sky. Faint traces of cloud hang there subtly in front the pale-blue backdrop. For Joe the new day's dawn represents the promise of yet another opportunity to which he is grateful. He props himself up, feeling better rested than he has since he was home and pulls himself out from under the tree. He sits beside it for a while and releases any nervous energy, toxic thought, and doubt in himself that he may have and absorbs his surroundings. He focuses on everything around him all at once but not for sounds that the hunter would make. For the moment, he chooses to see the forest for what it is and experience it in its natural state and not the dreadful setting the killer has made it.

This particular morning, he intends to embrace its beauty a little longer.

Before Joe heads out, he stops at a nearby puddle. It is shallow and clouds easily once disrupted, so he walks the immediate area and finds a bigger, deeper watering hole for which to utilize. He drinks from it, splashes his face, and runs his wet fingers through his hair. Once satisfied, he sets out northbound and strides along confidently.

Joe travels with a calculated efficiency, stopping briefly when necessary to rest. Sometimes he sits down, sometimes he leans on something, and other times he remains standing. No method is ever indulged in for too long. His determination to seize the day is too great.

Noon comes to pass, and as Joe advances forward, he hears a substantial shuffling behind him. Without taking a chance to glance back, he takes off like a bolt of lightning. His adrenaline skyrockets. He runs hard and fast and takes a beating from the woods as he does. He fights through brush, swerves around bushes, side-steps trees, and maneuvers himself up hills and down, all while avoiding protruding rocks, deep holes, and awkward intricacies within the earth. His ambition to evade the death that now obsesses for him and him alone is more prominent than ever. Joe must run, once again, until his feet can carry him no further.

Soon, he stumbles and falls awkwardly to his knees. He struggles to catch his breath, as he puts his hand over a cramp at his side, near his abdomen. The ground beneath him spins when he looks at it, so he averts his eyes upward to the sky as his heart rate slows.

Once he has collected himself, he looks forward, between the trees ahead and sees a large cluster of blended colors. There are splashes of reds, whites, and blues amongst the distant grass, below the trees. As his sight focuses in acutely, he observes more colors. In front is what looks like a wrought iron fence. It borders the wilds and separates them from a well-manicured flowerbed just beyond the tree line.

A different kind of beauty is there, outside the forest. There are shades of yellow, orange, pink, and purple nearby the red, white, and blue that had first caught his eye. There is cut green grass and perfectly trimmed hedges within the adjacent landscape. The scenery there is tame and organized. A view much cleaner than that of the wilderness. He is hesitant to trust his eyes and questions the sight, for what is out there beyond the forest, between the tree branches and leaves, terrifies him. But only for a fleeting moment and so, he closes them, inhales deep, tilts his head back and releases his breath to the sky.

Joe opens them and rises to his feet. He is wobbly at first, as he jogs to the forest's edge toward the streaks of color that divides the woods from a man-made clearing that is a stunning, and vast front courtyard. He impulsively jumps the fence. It surrounds an enormous ten thousand square-foot castle style mansion and lines approximately fifty thousand square feet of well-maintained property. It looks like a work of art; a panoramic centerfold, ripped from the pages of an upper-crust, European home and garden magazine's feature article. He takes a few steps forward and scans the impressive colossal building, left to right. It has four tall stories built with large, beige, rustic-style solid blocks below a heavily pitched network of rooftops and dormers with mahogany shaded ceramic shingles. The building is extremely wide and has matching stone towers at all four corners of its structure, as well as three main ones at the center, the middle one being the tallest. They stand as the modern-day castle's most prominent feature and dwarf the other four. Black bars cover numerous elegantly crafted windows that match the estate's lavish gates and lengthy fencing. There are flawless gardens laid out in the courtyard with great symmetry and elaborate flowerbeds perfectly lining the building. There are giant sculptures, artistically crafted birdbaths, and grand patio sets. A large red-brick driveway starts off from the left, out of Joe's view, and runs up a gradual hill as it curves around an outbuilding and a row of arborvitae trees to carry along the front of the buildings west side. It continues on by the front door's alluring stoop. It encircles a giant fountain with three tiers, which has on top a larger-than-life statue of a female. She is a figure from Greek mythology. Due to a leisurely interest with the subject, he is knowledgeable enough to know that it is none other than Athena, the goddess of war herself.

Joe cannot believe his eyes as he looks upon the paradise before him. To his right, he sees countless antique automobiles in pristine condition strewn about in front of the east wing of the impressive mansion: A 1925 blacked-out, lowered, Rolls Royce Phantom; a white 1933 Ford three-window coupe; and a silver 1948 Porsche 356.

Further to the right is an enormous open car garage filled to capacity with expensive, beautiful machines of all types. He is hypnotized by all that he surveys, as he scans the front of the building again, this time, right to left. Before he can even think of his next move, he spots movement to his far left, up at the top level of the west wing tower. It's a man dressed in a fine black suit standing at an opening. He shoots a rifle squarely aimed at Joe. He is struck with a Curaratura dart in the left side of his neck. The dart has a small bright orange tuft of feathers that protrude out of the end opposite his neck. Instantly, another dart hits his right shoulder. Before Joe can reach up to feel for what had hit him, he collapses on the front lawn and lays there still. He is unconscious.

Soon after, the two dapper, identically dressed young men who shot Joe appear in the courtyard from the east and west towers and approach him diagonally from his flanks. They meet up at the same time and stand on each side of their victim. They lift him up from under his shoulders. Joe's head hangs down toward his chest and his feet drag behind his body as the men carry him toward the mansion.

# 26

# Methods of Mayhem

A few hours later…

Joe wakes up dazed from his unconscious state. A fog in which, as he collects himself, it becomes clear that he has experienced some paralysis.

He brings his bound hands to his neck. His arms feel heavy and numb as he rubs the tiny scab where he was stuck with the first dart. Joe is in the corner of a small room, no bigger than the shacks scattered within the forest beyond the fences of the estate. It is dingy and appears to be a janitor's store area. It smells musty and of bleach. The finished concrete floor is cold and painted thick with a gray gloss enamel.

From where he lies, stuffed near the corner with the mops and buckets, Joe squints to see a basic table-and-chair set. A bright light hangs plainly from the center of the ceiling directly over top of it, illuminating some coffee mugs and overfilled ashtrays. The rest of the room is dim, all except the lit-up table. Upon further inspection, Joe notices that two of the mugs are steaming upward ever so slightly from inside. He inspects his hands. They are bound at the wrists with a black zip-tie; he fidgets with it, until he hears voices from outside the room. They grow increasingly louder. The door flies open.

He shuts his eyes and remains still.

"What are you saying?"

"I'm saying, this place is *so* big... Much bigger than his place in Switzerland."

"You'll do fine."

"Hopefully... I'd hate to get lost in here."

"Well, you haven't yet."

"It's only been a *couple of weeks*."

The two men from the towers sit at the table.

"I don't know what to tell you, Vincent..."

"Alright, alright...so go on, Kent, what happened to the other guy?"

"Emile? He retired, he was even older than Mr. Emmlington, if you can believe it."

"Oh, yeah, I think you told me that."

"Anyway...once this joker's out of here, things will pretty much return to normal... Mr. Emmlington will probably sleep a few days and then head on out."

"Where from here?"

"Not sure. *One* of his palaces."

"I see, so what happens right now *with us*, exactly?" asks Vincent.

"Well, we throw him in the back seat of the limo. We shot him twice, so he'll be conked out for another couple hours. Plenty of time to administer the antidote and dump him at the airport. How long you been in Mr. Emmlington's employ, anyway?" asks Kent, sarcastically.

"Comin' on three years, you know that."

"Yeah, I do, but you're acting like a complete greenhorn, you've been briefed on this stuff... Prepped...right? You should know everything about all the procedures by now."

"Well...yeah, but this last part seemed pretty messed up all the times I studied it. Besides, give me a break, I've never *actually* participated before."

"Yeah, yeah," says Kent.

"Was his last one in Switzerland?" inquires Vincent.

"Nah, not sure where and stop interrupting, where was I? Oh, yes, the airport! So, when he wakes up, first thing he'll do is find the cash, and the theory goes, rather than play detective, he'll buy a ticket, board the plane and figure it out on his way home… Or at least try to. Case closed. We'll never see him again. Apparently, it has never failed."

"Man, Emmlington's got a hell of an imagination to conjure this up!"

"Yeah, or just enough money to pull it off."

"You've been on a *couple* of these before, right?"

"Yep, six years ago in Wales and nine years ago in Belgium…for the most part it was same shit, different pile. Although in Belgium, he had a hunting partner, a real character this fuckin' guy. 'The Judge' they'd call him…think his name was 'Halliwell'…a larger-than-life type. A great big man…giant blustery pompous ass type. A blowhard. Anyway, he handled his business much quicker back then, even in Wales, without Judge." Kent shrugs. "Who knows why. He *was* a little younger after all. Perhaps his efficiency has finally slipped. But I had heard these guys proved particularly difficult too. And it should have been wrapped up sooner, I mean, I don't mind the overtime though…and being back in my home country 'n all."

"Ever feel bad?" asks Vincent.

"Nah, Mr. Emmlington keeps us ridiculously well paid. The money feels too good for anything else to feel bad," says Kent with a laugh.

"Yeah, that's the truth. I've heard that he's, like, one of the wealthiest men in the world."

"Maybe, but you won't find him on any Forbes list. According to media, he doesn't exist... His whole life is like a big *secret* or something. A mystery. Go online. I've tried and tried to find something, anything on the internet about him, but there is absolutely nothing."

"I've heard that. Crazy. So... what about the regular in-house staff? When should they return from *vacation*?" Vincent puts up two fingers from each hand and bobs them downward to accentuate the word '*vacation*' as he says it.

"Three days after we drop this guy," answers Kent while pointing a thumb sideways toward Joe, who's still playing dead.

"For now, it's just you and me and Mr. and Mrs. E. Speaking of which, we got a job to do. You go bring the limousine around front, and I'll meet you back here."

"You got it!" replies Vincent. He gets up without hesitation and leaves the room to fulfil his directive.

Kent lights up an extra-slim, extra-long, dark-brown cigarette and leans back in his chair as he smokes it. Joe opens his eyes ever so slightly. He notices that his shoes have been changed to new ones and his clothes are new too. He wears a fresh pair of blue jeans and a crisp, white long-sleeved shirt. His shank, gutter spikes, and water bottle are gone, and he has been cleaned right up. His hair and beard are tidy, and his wounds have been sterilized. He studies Kent.

Shortly thereafter, Vincent returns.

"All set," he says loudly. Kent extinguishes his cigarette and stands up.

Joe feigns unconsciousness perfectly. Vincent grabs his ankles, and Kent grabs him under his shoulders. The men carry him down a long, dark hallway, up a set of stairs, and out a door at the mansion's east wing. Vincent struggles with taking

Joe out through the doorway as he walks backwards. They manage to get outside, where a green Land Rover is parked in the driveway parallel to the door.

"Where's the limo?" asks Kent.

"Couldn't find it," answers Vincent. "Will this do?"

"Shit man, what the fuck?... I suppose it will, but never divert from the plan! The windows aren't privacy-tinted, fuck! If Mr. Emmlington asks... Ah, fuck it! He won't ask or even see us, he's up on the fourth floor."

The men set Joe in behind the driver's seat and buckle him up. They sit him upright with his head flopped forward. Vincent jumps into the passenger seat, with Kent climbing into the drivers.

"Where's the bag?" asks Kent.

"Trunk," replies Vincent.

"NO, no, go grab it, put it on his lap. It'll make for a quicker drop...didn't you learn anything from the memo?"

"Hey, the memo didn't say anything about putting him in a utility room either, but we did *that*."

"I *told* you," says Kent in exasperation, "we went through all this! The fucking guy wasn't supposed to stumble into the yard. That's *never* happened. I don't know *how* he didn't trip the perimeter alarm. James, Alan, Ethan, and Starks were gonna keep watch from the corner towers. The men slated to do *our* jobs usually go with Emmlington while he hunts the last fool down with his fucking dart gun and the doc in tow. I don't even have a key to the hospital section on my ring and even if I *did*, I wouldn't know what the fuck to do in there other than help restrain him. For fuck sakes, we're part-time, million-dollar errand boys. Depending on the day, we guard the estate or we chauffeur. Other than *this* thing, there's not a whole lot of responsibility for the money! You should just be glad we didn't have to carry this idiot on a fuckin' stretcher all through the woods. It's fuckin' awful."

"I simply don't understand why Mr. Emmlington didn't call the doctor back as soon as he found out we bagged the guy, so he could be properly monitored and evaluated before his release as stated in the plan."

"Because he couldn't be bothered. He's very tired and the boss wants nothing more to do with this shit 'till the next one in '15. Hell, Dr. Nokori was in the guest house for *days* waiting and I don't blame the little prick for leaving. What surprises *me* is that Mr. E doesn't have his men shoot to kill, should any of these guys breach surveillance, wander onto the property and discover the place, like this asshole did. Anyway, we were ordered to clean him up some, watch him a bit and then make the drop, so that's what we're doing."

Vincent shakes his head side to side, jumps out and goes around to the back of the S.U.V. After a moment, Kent finds the latch and pops the trunk, Vincent grabs the piece of luggage and comes around to the backside opposite Joe, opens the door, and rests it on his lap.

"Reconfigure him, will ya?" orders Kent. "Put his head back and pull his hips out so it *stays* leaning back. We don't need him looking fucking dead on the Interstate."

"What if he wakes?"

"He won't alright! I know my chemicals, we're good."

Vincent resituates Joe to a more natural-seated position and closes the door. He walks around to the passenger side and gets back in beside Kent. They drive down the long, winding driveway. About halfway down, the vehicle goes over a bump as the path turns from red brick to black tarmac. Kent turns on the radio; the low sounds of Andrea Bocelli and Sarah Brightman's classic duet '*Time to say Goodbye*' fill the Land

Rover. When they arrive at the gate, Kent hits a remote control clipped to the sun visor. It doesn't budge. He presses it again.

"Awe, what the hell?" says Kent. He looks over to Vincent who shrugs. "Holy shit man, I guess I'll do it myself." He unbuckles his seatbelt and as he moves to get out of the Land Rover, the cross-section of the seatbelt gets hung up on something underneath his suit jacket. "Fuck!" he yells as he reaches to the breast of his jacket to reveal a shiny Colt forty-five caliber handgun. Joe, steadily watching forward through narrow slits in his eyelids, remains still. Kent puts the gun on the center console's armrest.

"Chrome?" asks Vincent.

"My nickel-plated burner," replies Kent in a slow, sinister tone of voice. "Don't touch it," he snaps playfully.

"Nice," says Vincent of the pistol with a laugh. Kent walks about fifteen feet down the lane to the gate and begins to fumble with its main clasp. Vincent and Joe look on. Joe's eyes slowly move downward to the gun. In a flash, he snatches it with his bound hands and points the end of the barrel an inch from Vincent's temple.

He spots the safety and quickly releases it. He is counting on the gun being loaded and cocks it. Vincent slowly turns to Joe with an expression of pure shock. Joe's face is blank. He hesitates for just a second before pulling the trigger. Vincent's head explodes and his body falls toward his door. Blood-spatters coat the entire passenger side window and half the dashboard. Kent hears the shot and turns toward the vehicle, squinting heavily to see which one of them wields the weapon. Joe points the pistol at him. The men lock eyes. Joe's are determined, while terror fills Kent's. Three blasts sound off, one after the other. The bullets slip through the windshield and into Kent's chest. Joe exits the vehicle as he falls to the ground.

He walks up and stands over him, he watches as Kent rapidly succumbs to death. Joe frisks his body. He quickly flips through the dead man's wallet and puts it in his back pocket. He searches further and finds a butterfly knife in his boot. He cuts his ties, pockets the knife, and drags the body a short distance to the grass. He then walks back toward Vincent's body. He pulls it out of the Land Rover, onto the tarmac, and off the driveway. He searches it and finds a nine-millimeter blue, steel Glock seventeen fitted with a silencer. He presses both safeties on his new weapons and puts them in his jeans, at both hips. He then uncovers a wallet and pockets it too. Joe jumps back in the vehicle, kicks out the busted windshield, and drives fast through the iron gates. They pop open with relative ease upon impact. He continues about five yards down the driveway to a dirt road and stops. He squeezes the steering wheel in his fists and looks both ways. To his immediate left is a fenced-in dead end, filled with lush vegetation. His only obvious option is to turn right and drive like a bat out of hell to safety. He examines the road that leads to freedom. It cuts straight through the densely wooded area, dividing the unforgiving forest and carries on as far as the eye can see. He, then, turns his head from the right side and stares straight ahead across the road and into the open woods.

The scenery is all too familiar. He looks in the rear-view mirror to the mansion.

Joe slowly does a three-point turn and heads back up the driveway.

# 27

# Liberation

Joe looks at the door the deceased men had carried him out of as he drives past it and parks by the pronounced threshold at the front of the mansion. He walks a few steps up the cobblestone stairs to the slate rock landing. The over-sized nine-foot tall double doors are beautiful, in solid teak. The center where they meet are lined with detailed carvings of maple leaves intertwined with thick braided rope. He studies the large iron knockers that symmetrically adorn the majestic main entranceway. The one on the left is a female, a lioness, and on the right is a male lion with a lustrous mane. They are especially intriguing; atop their heads, the lioness wears a modest tiara while the lion has a flamboyant crown on, with sharp points.

Joe is somewhat surprised when he pushes on the doors and they sway open easily.

He walks slowly inside to an incredibly spacious, elegant foyer and looks around the grand room in astonishment. Every square inch has been designed and constructed with the utmost elite craftsmanship and the highest quality of building materials. The furnishings are just as impressive. It's the most stunning, lavish place he's ever been in. The space before him has eighteen-foot high, bright white ceilings that hang above emerald green marble floors and they are bordered by flawless, tan-colored walls with gold trimmings. On them are dark-stained, high baseboards, wide window casings, and thick chair rails. The mansions interior design is largely made up of old, exorbitant, Victorian style with an unconventionally combined influence of earthy flare.

There are giant works of classic art with extravagant gold frames hung all over and a six-foot portrait of the mustached man himself above a huge fireplace mantel, up ahead and off to Joe's left, directly across from a grand staircase and railing. It is the hunter, and he appears decades younger. His now-infamous facial hair is still prominent but smaller and darker in the painting.

In front of the fireplace is a large glass table. On its center is a tall vase, three feet high with swirls of gold and blue.

There is a chessboard made of speckled quartz with yellow and white gold pieces facing each other from opposite sides. The two armies timeless in their stances are set and ready for a strategic battle.

The walls are lined sporadically with beautiful antique dressers and hutches and on top them, are meticulously placed priceless trinkets of varying themes.

A teal carpet marks the path that runs along the front wall of the beautiful vestibule and carries along to other parts of the mansions main level. They flow from the front doors to the left, past the wall with the fireplace, through a wide hallway, and to the right to an identical corridor. The carpet also leads ahead of Joe, from where he stands at the entrance. It curves to the right and leads to the luxurious extra wide staircase. The steps ascend and curve heavily to the right as they reach the next level. Joe follows them up and around the bend. It leads to the second-floor hallway, where the carpet transitions from teal-blue to blood red. Across the corridor, the staircase continues and winds around and up to the mansion's next floor. Joe crosses the hallway and follows the steps up and around again and again, spanning one more corridor and two more flights, until he reaches the fourth floor. The hunter has become the hunted. His instincts tell him to walk the hallway of the west wing first in search of his enemy, for no more reason than that was the side of the building from which he noticed movement in the tower before he was brought down.

The walls are covered with vintage style, velvet wallpaper of brown, green and blue paisley and there are antique oil paintings along each side. As Joe walks quietly, he can't help but look at some of them. They vary in subject matter. Most are landscapes, some are portraits, and others are more obscure. Each one is cased within an intricately designed gold frame. The paintings with wilderness themes especially frustrate him. One art piece in particular catches his eye over the rest. He stops a moment on the red carpet that follows along the center of the heavily glazed, solid-oak floor. It is the late Russian painter, Ivan Aivazovsky's masterpiece, 'The Ninth Wave.' In it, there is a small group of men on an open ocean clinging for life on a detached mast from a ship as it drifts aimlessly on the ferocious, unforgiving surface. The vessel is not there, and the bright yellow sun is hung beyond the tall, crashing waves in the distant horizon. It interests him greatly that the main subject of the image is not actually seen, but merely suggested. Not the ship, nor the disastrous scenario to which it likely sunk is shown and neither is their impending destiny. The painting depicts a powerful moment frozen in time between two arguably more important others. Though it appears somewhat obvious at a glance, the situation is but a mystery. Whatever *had* happened, he hopes all the men had made it and been saved.

Joe carefully continues. He stops every time he gets to one of the many doors and listens close, putting his ear to each one with both guns drawn. He waits a moment before passing. He cannot make any sound that would result in a mishap, so pays close attention to his movements and reigns in his breathing.

If so much as a floorboard were to creak, it could blow his cover. His heart rate slows as he methodically searches for signs of his tormenter. After what seems like a mile and listening through several identical closed oak doors along the west wing, he reaches the end of the long hallway and doubles back to scour the opposite side of it. One after the other comes and goes, until he arrives at a door that is open an inch or so. He looks behind himself before intently listening by. He doesn't hear a sound and enters the room; there is no one there. He holsters his Colt forty-five in the backside of his jeans at the small of his back, but keeps the Glock in hand.

The room is big in scale and extremely long.

Joe is both fascinated and terrified when he sees countless uniformed mannequins on both sides of the room. They are lined up into two long rows and each row is parallel and facing one another in perfect symmetry within the otherwise empty space. Each uniform is worn by a plain-faced mannequin that stands posed on a four-foot high, cherry wood base, with an engraved gold plate mounted front and center, to its top-side. Joe follows the row to his right.

The first uniform he analyzes is that of Roman Garb. The engraving reads:

CALIGULA, 'THE PERVERT CAESAR'
~ ROMAN EMPEROR 37 AD – 41 AD

The uniforms are perfect replicas. Joe explores further.

The second base reads:

GENGHIS KHAN, 'THE SUPREME WARRIOR'
~ FOUNDER AND RULER OF THE MONGOL EMPIRE 1206 – 1227

Joe observes for a few seconds and continues.
He looks at the third one:

HENRY VIII, 'THE BLUEBEARD KING'
~ KING OF ENGLAND 1509 – 1547

…and the fourth:

IVAN IV, 'THE TERRIBLE'
~ TSAR OF ALL RUSSIA 1533 – 1584

*Someone is quite obviously seriously into tyrants, dictators, and the most evil of historic leaders,* thinks Joe. He feels queasy in his stomach.

The fifth one is:

JOSEPH STALIN, 'THE FATHER OF NATIONS'
~ GENERAL SECRETARY OF THE SOVIET UNION 1922 – 1953

Joe gets particularly sickened when he gets to the sixth uniform:

ADOLF HITLER, 'THE FUHRER'
~ SUPREME CHANCELLOR OF GERMANY
1933 – 1945

Joe thinks of Roebuck, and when he found the killer's rifle and recalls the Nazi German outfit he was wearing as he murdered his friend in cold-blood. Joe is overcome with sorrow. The emotion quickly turns to anger. He crosses the room as if to evade his anxiety, only for it to chase him and come flooding back instantly. He stands in front of another replica:

POL POT, 'BROTHER NUMBER ONE'
~ RULER OF KAMPUCHEA 1975 – 1979

He can't shake the thoughts of his friends being stalked and murdered and quickly decides that he's just about had enough of the sinister display. He strides fast, passing Kaiser Wilhelm the 2$^{nd}$, Mao Tse-tung, and Augusto Pinochet.

He walks until, from his peripheral, he notices a long-flowing royal blue cape, richly embroidered with gold thread. He skips some of the other uniforms for a closer look. Upon inspection, he examines The sash, and tunic with it's red collar and matching sleeve-cuffs, the golden sword, baggy white trousers and polished black boots. The engraved plate on its base indicates that it's the Mexican tyrant Santa Anna's uniform.

Joe's adrenaline soars as the stories Charlie had told of a man in a royal blue cape, shooting Neil dead from afar quickly make their way to the forefront of his mind. A murder that had prompted Charlie's ill-fated jump from the cliff where he would later be discovered, heavily injured at the bottom, below a juniper bush by Joe himself. His head spins. As he looks over every piece of the uniform, he is disgusted to find some runs in the fabric at the cape's bottom end and fragments of dead

Burr-bush embedded into it. He grimaces in anguish and exits the room.

Joe continues east down the west hallway with his Glock seventeen drawn. He listens by the next door on his right… There is no sound. He stops at the next door. It is slightly ajar. He listens for a moment. Just as he decides to move on, he hears a faint shuffling from within and is frozen in his tracks.

He puts his ear near the door and listens again. More indistinguishable sounds emit softly from inside the room.

Joe is intimidated at first but recalls his friends and begins to fume with passionate anger. Any and all weakness he had felt from his time in the forest is gone. He pushes the door open and slowly enters the room with his Glock held straight out and pointed in front of him, he cradles the stock with his other hand.

J. Oskar Emmlington is sitting at a desk across from him as plain as day. Composed, he looks up to Joe from a map he's been studying. His face goes flush and he perks up.

The daylight makes the large-paned glass window behind Oskar glow white.

It's another long room. It is a smoking lounge. There is glass cabinetry to Joe's immediate left and leather-bound furniture scattered all over within the large space to the right.

Joe looks like he is staring at a ghost, one that's haunted and terrorized his very soul… And now here he is, sitting right there before him.

"Ahhh, it's the winner," says Oskar in a British Received Pronunciation style accent with an interesting German hochdeutsch influence and a slight twist of southern United States, white vernacular.

The statement catches Joe off-guard.

"Th…the…winner?" he repeats.

"What kind of game would it be if there were no winner?" Oskar's statements leave Joe's mind reeling. He plants his feet, as his hand drops from the butt of his pistol but he keeps his arm extended and the silenced barrel pointed at his adversary.

"You see my boy, years ago, back before some of my closest business associates…my friends…before they died, they would be very much involved…as much as I. We'd all buy into the contest at the same price and each pick a *horse,* if you will. For every elimination, a score was tallied. A point a kill. We'd even place side wagers on a chosen package, depending on this or that allocated variable they possessed, be it natural or given. The competitor with the highest score got the pot, and the last subject standing would fetch a prize from his sponsor." The divulgence of information comes at Joe fast. He is disturbed to hear the explanation of his abduction and sickened by the way his captor so nonchalantly unpacks it. He cannot believe the audacity of what is being disclosed and his anger builds by the second. "That last subject, *you* in this case," says Oskar as he perks up again and points at Joe, "have won the most in a way. You've won back your life! And a handsome sum of your own of course, sort of a…participation bonus for your trouble. The loser of the game, amongst the betting men, was the man with the lowest amount of points. He must then surrender a previously determined donation which would have been paid dutifully to the aforementioned winning subject, who was then subsequently set free. So," Oskar takes a quick breath, "for the most part, everyone would remain as honorable as could be and so forth." He stops and stares off, in deep thought as he recalls times past, he then shakes his head from side to side as he arrives back at the present.

"Speaking of which, you received your prize money, I trust?" he asks, in a cavalier manner.

"Prize money." repeats Joe.

"Yes, ten million dollars... That's sufficient in this day and age, yes? I raised the pay-out this year."

"You!" Joe's rage kicks in. "You think you can buy me? Buy *us!*" he shouts.

"Quite the contrary, my boy. I already have...*twice*," replies Oskar. "Once, a long time ago, upon placing my order and again today... Today, I've bought the rest of your life, in cash! However, it isn't personal... It could have been anybody. You should consider yourself lucky and, furthermore, be proud of yourself for making it through. Now, lower that pistol..."

"Why are you telling me all this?" urges Joe.

"You're pointing a gun at me," answers Oskar. "A gun that you had better lower, however... We don't want problems, do we?"

"Problems!" shouts Joe. "You're sick! You're absolutely fuckin' twisted!"

"A bit eccentric, a bit mad even, but twisted? *Sick*? No," says Oskar.

"Do you have any idea what you've done to us?"

"Young man, I'm quite aware. After all, I was there, you know."

"It's Joe! My name is Joe!"

"Yes, yes. I read the dossier," says Oskar. "You need to lower your weapon before things get dicey!" he adds, as he tightens his grip on the gold-plated, double-barreled sawed-off shotgun that is hanging from a brass swivel hook, installed underneath the surface of his desk. He slowly turns it toward Joe.

The nameplate above, on the front and center edge of his oppressor's desk, reads:

Diederich Jaeger Fleisher

"Your men called you Emmlington?"

Oskar sees him eyeing the tag and to what Joe is referring. "My father was English, but my beloved mother was German. Diederich Jaeger are my given names, and Fleisher is my mother's maiden name. But for business, J. Oskar Emmlington has such a better ring, doesn't it?" he asks rhetorically, with a sigh. "It was my father's last name, and I just dropped the 'Diederich' all together and put the 'J' from 'Jaeger' in front of Oskar, a name I always thought was appealing," he finishes his explanation, as if bored by the topic.

"Now, speaking of my men," says Oskar, "where are they?"

He sits up in his chair, further revealing his casual attire. He's wearing a matching outfit: a tan pair of trousers and collared shirt. His wide-brimmed hat is rolled up and tied on one side. He adjusts his ascot.

"Why us?" yells Joe as he motions to the window. "Why *people*?"

"Oh, it's nothing… It's just sport, m'boy," says Oskar rather complacently.

"And you've done this before? Brought human beings out to the middle of nowhere? To hunt them!" exclaims Joe.

"Indeed, and I have a very particular formula for it," he adds proudly. "I strive to indulge in it, every three years and have done it for decades. The locations change on a rotating loop throughout every viable place I own, all over the globe… And I have many places," says Oskar smartly.

"How do you get away with this?" yells Joe, nudging his pistol firmly toward Oskar. Joe resists the urge to pull the trigger. He must have more closure.

"When you're a man of such wealth and power as I, you can buy anything," says Oskar. "The lucky seven, taken from all over the country, almost simultaneously, is almost impossible to tie together. No evident motive. The people, of course, must be…average Joes," he says with a sinister grin and malice in his voice. "There are factions of professionally organized criminals that do this kind of work every day. If anyone were to ever sniff around, which nobody does, millions of dollars smell very good, wouldn't you agree? Did you know that there are hundreds of thousands of missing people in America alone, about whom the authorities have NO leads? C'mon my boy," says Oskar. "Smarten up!"

"How many," demands Joe. "How many have you imprisoned? And murdered!" he shouts.

"Well, imprisonment and *murder* are merely points of view… But that's a talk for another time."

"How many!" yells Joe again, now furious.

"I haven't done the math… It wouldn't take all that long, but I couldn't be bothered. I *will* tell you this… See that open safe in the wall behind me?" Oskar points back behind himself with his thumb without looking.

"It's a human skull," whispers Joe. He is horrified. Amidst the rush of confronting his oppressor and the bright light of the uncovered window, he hadn't noticed it.

"My first kill! Well…*hunted* kill," says Oskar. "1985… Here, on *these* very grounds," he says as he taps his map with his index finger. "Ironically enough, his name was Joe too. Now, I take no interest in my catches' names, but like I said, it was my first!"

"What do you do with the bodies?" asks Joe in disgust.

"It depends…my men handle them, the animals take care of them too, from time to time…and sometimes the subjects take care of themselves or each other. Did you happen to come across any stray skeletons in the wild? I've always wondered that about you people."

Joe is astonished. "Do you take women or children?" he asks with persistence and widening eyes.

Oskar laughs. "*That* hunt would be a trifle easy. No, no, just men... There's one-hundred-and-fifty square miles of untouched acreage out there and countless lakes. Only full-grown males will do."

As his emotions run wild, it dawns on Joe that he hasn't even asked where he is. Before he can inquire, Oskar continues...

"Did you know that this part of America contains the largest continuous area of uncut forest remaining in the United States? A hell of a place to get lost, is it not?" he asks rhetorically with sly condescension, as a way to further patronize and toy with his subject. "I just *adore* the wilds of Minnesota."

Joe is stunned, by the reveal from his sinister captor. His head swims.

"You can't get anywhere on foot from those woods, ya know. I'm certain it's impossible. Especially for a common man of this era. Even *if* I lost track of you, you'd eventually succumb to death...wandering, in vain... And even *if* you got to the road...it's far too long to walk it all the way out, and besides, it's my road anyway. You *truly* are in the middle of nowhere."

"And yet here I am...with you."

"Indeed, you are..." Oskar grins. "Now, all winners of this contest are put back far richer than they were, and we never hear of them again. If you choose not to do the same, I'll gladly take back my generous donation and your miserable life with it," he says calmly and with a wry smile.

Joe can't comprehend how, even in the face of his own demise, the killer could be so arrogant.

"You are crazy," he says.

"It's possible," returns Oskar.

"Tell me one more thing."

"Certainly…"

"Why do you do this? *Why?*"

Oskar doesn't hesitate. "The *thrill*," he answers, coldly, reveling in the word as he over-enunciates it.

"Now, before you tell me where my men are, I shall leave you with this—"

Joe interrupts, "And what about the getups? Why do you wear the uniforms?"

Oskar laughs. "A bit of a boyhood fantasy come alive, I suppose," his voice steadily rises… "Now, you said one more question when in fact that was two! I have had just about enough!" he says, quite irritated. "When presented with the most difficult of obstacles, one if at all possible, must persevere to become a better version of oneself…"

"And who the fuck are *you* to tell me that!" shouts Joe.

"My men!" shouts Oskar, even louder.

"DEAD!" yells Joe. "Dead and in hell! You'll see them soon enough!" he declares as he steadies his arm to gun Oskar down.

Just before Joe pulls the trigger, Oskar speaks, "A pity about my desk."

Suddenly, Oskar unloads his shotgun, blowing a huge hole out of the front of his desk. Bullets scatter. A few shards of wood catch Joe's legs as shrapnel peppers the wall and door behind him. He is sent backwards. The Glock goes flying. His knees give out and he falls hard onto his rear-end and over on his back. His Colt forty-five has come out of his jeans and lies just beside him by his left ankle on a large spatter of blood. Oskar rises and calmly walks to his right to the set of glass cupboards above a matching cabinet.

He searches inside for a weapon and locates a gold fifty-caliber Smith and Wesson model 500 revolver.

Joe is scrambling for the forty-five.

Oskar checks the chamber, it is fully loaded. As he turns around to finish the job, Joe grabs his gun in the nick of time and quickly shoots Oskar four times fast. Once in the hip, once in the stomach, and twice in the chest.

Oskar looks down at Joe in astonishment. He drops the gaudy handgun and grabs his stomach, clutching his fresh wounds. He examines his red, blood-soaked hands and his hat falls off in front of him and down to the floor, revealing his disheveled, thinning hair. He's bleeding profusely from his four bullet holes as he stumbles backwards and crashes into the counter, breaking the glass and severely cutting himself in several places. He pushes for a moment, into the floor with his boot heels and against the broken cabinet as to stand himself up from his lean and instead loses his footing, slicing his body further on the large shards of glass and imbedding himself down deeper into the cabinetry. He watches in sheer terror from his back as Joe rises.

He picks up the golden fifty-caliber magnum and tosses the Colt toward the door, landing it beside the Glock. Oskar struggles to breathe. Blood gurgles up from his esophagus, through his throat and splashes out from his mouth as Joe towers over him in all his glory.

"It's evil men!" he shouts. "And wicked souls that *fight* to keep this world in darkness!" Joe's eyes are blazing. "And today, on behalf of all those boys you've MURDERED! You shall receive our vengeance."

Joe unloads the magnum into Oskar's face until it is gone and tucks the golden gun into the backside of his bloody jeans along the small of his lower back. He steps over to the desk, folds up the map and puts it in his back pocket. He then goes to the wall beside the window, removes a small tapestry and lays it out flat on the desk. He carefully takes the anonymous man's skull from the safe, places it on its center, joins the four corners of the tapestry together and twists them up, creating a makeshift sack. He eyes a blunderbuss mounted lengthways on the wall by the doorway across from the desk for just a moment and then looks down to a British uniform slung over an armchair below. The red coat and white sash, along with a grass-stained pair of white pants, appear battered. A black cocked hat sets atop a pair of ruined, black leather long boots on the floor nearby an end table with a Calabash pipe on top of it. He sets the bag over his shoulder and limps back through the door he came in from.

Moments later, Joe exits the front doors of the mansion. He hobbles directly toward the S.U.V and opens the driver-side door. He pauses as he spots the 1925 Rolls Royce Phantom in the corner of his eye. Joe shuts the door and looks the classic car over. He walks to the backside of the Land Rover and grabs the duffle bag of money from the back seat. He opens it and carefully puts the bundled tapestry inside, on top of numerous stacks of bound thousand-dollar bills and zips it up. As he shuffles back along the driveway toward the east wing of the building, he stops in his tracks. Joe sees an elderly woman knelt down before a flowerbed in the side-yard at the northeast corner, just beside the house. It is Oskar's wife. She has on a large, plain straw hat with a wide white silk ribbon tied around it and is wearing a thin, subtly colored, floral-patterned summer dress. She has long yellow gardening gloves on her hands and digs into the earth with them. Joe slings the duffle bag over his shoulder, takes his gun from his back, and holds it up offensively in front of himself at eye level. With bended elbow and his finger on the trigger, he stares at the tip of the golden barrel, pointed toward to the sky. It gleams under the summer sunshine.

He looks back at the woman, who has stopped gardening to acknowledge two identical hummingbirds that have decided to pay her a visit. She carefully takes off her gloves and sets them down. She smiles big and bright below her hat as the birds move in wonderful, unified motions in front of her. They flutter and weave as she outstretches her arms and holds the palms of her hands out underneath them.

Joe looks back at his gun. A moment passes. He sets the firearm back behind himself and into the waist of his jeans. He looks at her again. She raises her hands closer to the tiny birds and slowly moves her fingers all around as they hover and dance above her aged hands.

Joe limps toward the pristine black Phantom. He opens the round driver's side door, jumps inside its red leather interior and sets the bag on the passenger seat. He is happy to see the keys dangling from the ignition and doesn't hesitate to fire up the classic machine's engine. It growls. There is a full tank of gas. He eases the clutch into gear and cruises slowly down the driveway. The woman does not see him.

Behind her, standing upright in the grass, within the frame of the car's rearview mirror, Joe notices the white cat, Hope. She is standing there, relaxed with her four legs together and her tail wrapped around her paws, she watches Joe leave. After a good look, he averts his eyes and peers through the windshield in front of him. He carefully steers the vehicle away from Vincent and Kent's bodies, stops at the end of the driveway briefly, and turns right. He does not check his side-mirrors or the rearview a second time. As he disappears down the road, he keeps his eyes directly forward and fixes his gaze straight ahead. Joe does not look back.

## End

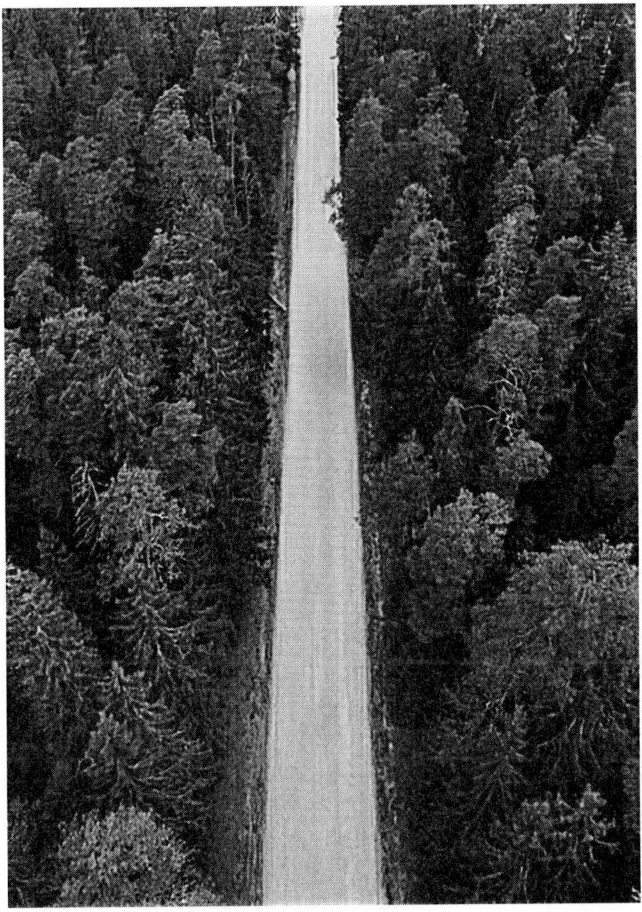